SEVERED INNOCENCE

In the old fishing trawler's hold, a rough sanitary room had been hastily fashioned with sheets of five mil plastic hung from the overhead on lengths of PVC pipe rigged for the occasion. In front of the room was a desk with what looked to be a game computer hooked to a thirty-two-inch monitor, one side of which was displaying the vitals of a very large man that was strapped to a hospital bed in the middle of the room. Directly over him was a high-intensity light normally used in an operating room, and to his right was an I.V. stand with bags of clear fluids that were being fed into his arm through tubes that terminated in the veins of his bruised forearm. His chest heaved slightly as the man struggled to breathe, and the only other sign of life was the chirping of the monitor that was connected to his body in several places.

Sitting at the desk and observing the monitor was a slender built man in his fifties with a hard look to his features, and in a chair next to him but facing the man on the bed was a heavy set man with the look of an over the hill prize fighter, complete with bent nose, cauliflowered ear, and thick set eyebrows growing haphazardly from ridges made up of mostly scar tissue.

"In the old days, I could have gotten the information that Julius needs from this pig in a few hours," the big man mumbled.

"Alas, Yuri, these are not the old days, and Julius doesn't want any marks on the body when we dump him," the slender man replied, "Why don't you go see what they are cooking tonight while I finish up down here. I'll meet you in the galley."

i

ISBN 978-0-9978186-5-9

Published by Purple Sage Entertainment, Hopkinsville, Kentucky

Printed in the United States of America on acid-free paper.

will@purplesageentertainment.com

W.W.Brock

brock@wwbrock.com

http://www.wwbrock.com

SEVERED INNOCENCE

BY

W.W. BROCK

DEDICATION

I would like to dedicate this book to my wife; the love of my life. Without her support and encouragement, I would not have started writing.

Prologue

Henry Albright, the man that the locals around Newcastle, Washington thought of as a reclusive sort, kept his business dealings quiet, even from his wife. His family knew him as 'Uncle Henry' and a man that they could count on for help in times of need. Hanna Albright Tucker, the wife of Michael Tucker, knew that 'Uncle Henry' was heavily involved in activities around the country that some would call shady at best and downright illegal at worst, but he was also the person that was responsible for hiding her and the family when she became a target by killing one of the most important members of the Los Zetas cartel.

This particular morning was like almost every other as Henry took his Jack Russell terrier, Sammy, out for their morning walk down the secluded road in the front of the cabin that he kept on the Lake near Priest River, Idaho. In the first glow of the predawn morning, Henry checked his surroundings before moving away from the cabin at a brisk walk. A big man, Henry had long since given up jogging for the more refined exercise of the quiet early morning walk with his dog, which would be followed by a hearty breakfast once they were back in the cabin.

As Sam explored the road just a few yards ahead of him, Henry watched and listened closely for any sign of the wolf pack that ran through the area from time to time, his right hand on the K-22 Smith and Wesson that he carried in his jacket pocket. Satisfied that they were alone on the road that was lit now by a cold morning pre-dawn light, Henry picked up his pace a bit to catch Sam, who was just out of sight at a bend in the road. Suddenly, after a brief bark of alarm, Sam yelped as if in pain, and Henry ran to where the dog was lying on the roadside with blood running from a small hole in his head.

As Henry knelt down, he felt a momentary sharp pain in his neck, and then his world went black.

CHAPTER ONE

The ringing of the cell phone startled Tuck out of a sound sleep, and it wasn't until he reached for the phone on his nightstand that the realization came to him that something was wrong. The phone that was ringing was a secure burner that the group was using for the highest level of emergencies. Tuck sprang to the dresser where that one was laying and picked it up.

"Get Hanna and the kids on a commercial flight tonight and meet me in Miami. They've got Henry," it was Shaun O'Brien's voice on the other end.

"Shaun, what is going on? Who has Henry?" Tuck asked, instantly awake.

"Tuck, we need to assume the worst until it's proven differently. If you can get moving before Henry cracks, assuming that he has been kidnapped, you might have a chance to save the family, but you need to go right now. Grab the IDs and clean out your stash, we'll come up with a plan at the safe house," O'Brien told him.

"On the way, Chief, see you in Miami," Tuck ended the call and turned to see Hanna sitting up in the bed staring at him.

"Tuck, what is it? What has happened to Uncle Henry?" Hanna seemed close to tears.

"I don't know yet, Hanna, but Shaun says for us to grab the emergency cash and get out of here tonight. I'll go get the passports while you get the kids. Just pack essentials, we've got enough money for clothes and things once we get there," Tuck told her.

"Where is there, exactly?" she asked.

"Miami, now get moving, we have a lot to do and no time to do it," he responded while moving to another room of the house.

Hanna moved quickly to the nursery and packed an overnight bag for the baby. Emily would be less of a problem since she liked to go at the drop of a hat and really didn't care where, as long as her daddy was with her. Baby Michael was a different story, though. Hanna was nursing and had him on a schedule for feeding that would no doubt be interrupted for the next few days until they could get settled again. She knew that her family was probably leaving Barbados for good, but right now any grief that she felt over that was outweighed by the need to protect her children at all costs.

Tuck collected the old cell phones and was about to throw them away when the burner rang again, "Go ahead, Shaun."

"Not Shaun, old buddy, Amos here. I just got the news and am headed for Kingston to stash the plane. Why don't you fly the family up with me, and we'll bum a ride in with some friends of mine there? It will keep us off of the radar for a while longer," Amos Whitehorse said.

"That might be a good idea since we don't have a clue what's happened. How much time can you give us?" Tuck asked.

"We should be out of here before dawn...say two hours tops. Can you make that?" he responded.

"Yes, we'll meet at the dock unless something happens," Tuck ended the call.

"What are we going to do now?" Hanna asked as she came into the room carrying the baby.

"We are going to fly to Kingston with Amos and pick up another ride from there. He didn't say what that would be," Tuck answered, "I'm going to book tickets for us to New York round trip. I've got a plan that might throw anybody looking for us off the scent for a while."

While Hanna threw some clothes for the kids in a small canvas bag, Tuck took a piece of luggage that they used for a carry-on and threw some old clothes and the cell phones in before shutting and locking it.

"I'll need your passport, Hanna. Something tells me that we won't be back here as George and Stephanie Alexander," Tuck told her.

"I had the same thought, Michael, and to tell the truth, I am relieved. It always felt like we were living a lie, and I worried about what we would tell the children when they got old enough to know," she answered.

"Well, we are going to have to use another set of passports for a short while so don't get too comfortable as Hanna Tucker just yet," he laughed, "Now, I am going to run to the airport and check this luggage through to New York, and I should be back in an hour. If not, head to the dock and wait for me on the plane with Amos."

"Aye, aye, Captain," she gave him her best salute followed by a hug, "Be careful."

The terminal was quiet except for a few tourists that were gathering for their homeward bound flight in a few hours, so Tuck headed for the empty Jet Blue counter, and the sleepy looking attendant.

"I'd like round trip tickets for my wife and I, and our two children to New York City on the first flight out, Ma'am," he told her.

"Certainly, Mister...?" she replied.

"Alexander, George Alexander, and my wife Stephanie," Tuck slid the passports across the counter, "My wife will meet me here with the children a little later. I was hoping to go ahead and check my luggage now if that would be possible."

"Of course, just let me get all of the information, and then I'll take care of your bag," she replied with a big smile.

Thirty minutes later and Tuck was headed back to the house to retrieve his family slowing only to pick up the burner phone and make a call to Shaun O'Brien.

"O'Brien," came the voice after one ring.

"Shaun, we've had a change of plans. I'm coming in with Amos through a contact in Kingston. We've booked a round trip to New York City and checked our cell phones in with the luggage," Tuck told him.

"Well, that is actually pretty good thinking, Tuck. How are you coming in?" Shaun asked.

"You know Amos better than I do. There is no telling what he has up his sleeve. Is the safe house still a go?" he answered.

"For now, I'll keep you updated on Henry as soon as my guys out there find anything...if they find anything. This doesn't look good," Shaun told him, "Tell Amos that we can't be any longer than two days meeting up. That will save me a phone call and a headache."

"Ten-four, I'll call when we reach Kingston," Tuck ended the call.

Hanna was ready to leave when he got home, and Emily ran out to jump in the front seat with her daddy.

"Where we go, Daddy?" she asked sweetly.

"For a little ride, Sugar, Uncle Amos is flying us someplace special," Tuck gave her a hug and passed her back to Hanna.

"I certainly hope that's true," he thought to himself as he watched Hanna taking care of the kids in the back seat.

CHAPTER TWO

A brand new SeaStar single-engine turboprop was taxiing to the end of the dock when Tuck and Hanna arrived in the parking lot. They hurried to board while there was no activity in the marina, managing to squeeze into the smaller plane with room to spare.

"Hey there Hanna," Amos greeted her as he helped Emily into the back of the plane, "There is a surprise for you inside."

"Hello Amos got some new wings, I see," Tuck shook his hand, "How soon can we get off this island?"

"Right away, why don't you sit up close to me so we can make a few plans," Amos suggested.

In the back, they heard Emily let out a squeal of delight, "Auntie Mags, Auntie Mags!"

Maggie O'Brien-Whitehorse gave Emily a big hug and then embraced Hanna as they moved to take seats in the smaller plane.

"Maggie, I certainly am happy to see you!" Hanna exclaimed as she found a seat for her and Tuck Junior.

"I'm so sorry to hear about Henry, Hanna. Amos and I decided that we would stick together until we find out what is going on. I've taken a leave of absence from Vanguard that should give us enough time," Maggie told her.

"I'm just glad to know that I'm not going to be the only woman on this trip, Maggie," Hanna replied with a smile.

"Buckle up back there," Amos told them, "We are leaving right now!"

He taxied the plane slowly out to the open water and shoved the throttle up on the seven hundred horsepower turboprop, ignoring protocol about calling in his departure to the local authorities.

"Shouldn't you tell them that we are leaving?" Tuck asked as the plane reached take off speed and climbed to an altitude of fifteen thousand feet.

"I doubt it will do more than irritate them. Besides, I don't think that we will be back here anytime soon, do you?" Amos responded, "I would also be very surprised if any of those boys even know what this is. Henry got the second one off the production line after that last job that we did for Interpol."

"How long to Kingston?" Tuck asked.

"About two hours. We'll have to go through a little customs check there, but those skids have been greased for us. I'm letting one of the government officials use the plane while we are gone," Amos laughed.

"Well, we can always buy it back at an impoundment auction once the guy gets popped for drug running," Tuck mused.

"There is always that, I suppose," Amos chuckled.

"Hanna, we will need the new IDs for Kingston. Have you got the brown wig with you?" Tuck turned and spoke to Hanna.

Emily was playing with Maggie so Hanna moved closer to his seat, "I hope you like Gerald and Adelaine Stokes, Jerry."

Tuck laughed, "Hopefully, this will not be needed in a few days."

"Oh, I don't know. Adelaine is kind of cute," she told him, "Little Rebecca and William is a stretch, though."

"Make sure that Emily...Rebecca knows her new name, at least until we get to Miami," Tuck told her.

Amos held the speed at two hundred and forty knots as they flew through the early morning sky toward Kingston, Jamaica. So far there was no sign of anyone following, but they all knew from experience that everything could change in a matter of minutes and that knowledge kept them on the edge of their seats for the two-hour flight.

Tuck had emptied the safe and was carrying ten thousand dollars in U.S. currency, twenty South African Krugerrands valued at just over twelve hundred dollars apiece in a belt under his shirt, and two Rolex watches which he and Hanna wore, but could be turned into ready cash. In addition, there was a safety deposit box in Miami that held new passports, twenty thousand dollars in currency, ten Rolexes, and twenty more Krugerrands that were his rainy day account, and, boy oh boy, it certainly looked like storm clouds were on the horizon!

Amos touched the sleek aircraft down just outside the harbor area at the Caribbean Maritime Institute and taxied slowly up the seventy-five-foot wide waterway behind the harbor until he reached a dock area where they were greeted by a tall dark skinned man in a white tropical suit and an unmistakable British accent. His men helped guide the plane into the dock after Amos secured the engine, and then he greeted them as they debarked.

"Ah, hello Amos. I trust you've had a pleasant flight?" he asked as he shook Amos' hand.

"Very nice, Reggie, very nice. You have met my wife, Maggie, and these are my friends, Gerald and Adelaine Stokes," Amos replied, "This is Reginald Smythe, Minister of Customs."

"And what is your name little one?" the man called Reggie asked Emily as she tried to hide behind Tuck.

"My name is Rebecca," she said shyly.

"Well, Miss Becky, welcome to our island paradise," Reggie replied.

"Not Becky! My short name is Becca!" she responded in what could have been taken as anger.

"I'm sorry for my daughter's outburst, Sir," Hanna apologized as she looked at Emily in surprise, "She is very particular about her name."

"I understand, my girls were very much like her at that age," Reggie said politely, "My men will take you to the Kinston airport where I have a diplomatic flight headed to Nassau in about thirty minutes. I understand that Amos has arranged for the last leg of your trip. Might I wish you a very pleasant...ahem...holiday?"

"Thank you so much, Mr. Smythe. Amos told me that you had taken a risk to help us, and I would like to thank you for that," Tuck said as he shook Reggie's hand with a Krugerrand palmed in his.

Reggie's eye grew wide as he realized what had transpired and a big grin crossed his face, "It has been my pleasure to be of service, Mister Stokes, my pleasure indeed."

Turning to Amos, he held out his hand and received the keys and paperwork for the SeaStar.

As Tuck and Hanna followed the men to another boat that was tied to the dock, they heard Reginald Smythe shout a loud, "Bon Voyage!"

CHAPTER THREE

The Cessna Citation II wasted no time in getting airborne once the passengers were inside and buckled up. Tuck glanced around the cabin of the luxuriously outfitted aircraft and noticed that the two men in the back of the plane appeared to have a military look to them. More so than he thought natural for Jamaican diplomats. Still that extra sense that he seemed to have when it came to smelling trouble wasn't active, so Tuck put the idea in the back of his mind and looked out of his window.

The plane was at cruising altitude now and the first thing that he noticed was that they were not headed in a Northerly direction, but ever so gradually making a turn to the west. Tuck caught Amos' eye and quietly gave him a sign that something was up. The response was a brief affirmative shake of the head as Amos casually got up and eased his way toward the flight deck.

"Hey you, up front. Where do you think you are going?" one of the men behind them shouted.

"Just stretching my legs is all. I have to use the can," Amos replied.

"Back here behind us," was the response from the other man.

"Thanks, Guys," Amos turned and made his way down the aisle toward the toilet.

Hanna gave Tuck a wide-eyed look and received a slight nod in return. She very quietly slid her hand into the bag that she was carrying and waited.

Amos came back down the aisle and slapped Tuck on the shoulder, "Boy that was a relief."

"I think that I need to relieve myself too, Amos," Tuck said as he stood, "Honey, I'll be right back."

He made his way past the two men that watched his every move and gave them a smile and a nod as he reached the toilet closet. Once inside, his right hand slid to the back of his waistband under his island shirt and came out with a Glock 42 in .380 caliber that almost always resided there, invisible in The Handgun Sling that he had picked up from a vendor in Florida, to all but closest scrutiny.

He opened the door outward and started to step into the cabin when he noticed that one of the men was not in his seat and was not visible. Since the door swung to his left, there was only one place the man could be, and that was behind the door. Tuck didn't hesitate. He knew that these mercenaries, because now it was apparent what they were, were expecting some type of trouble from him so he slammed the door open with his body and threw himself across the narrow aisle, swinging his right hand into position to make the shot on the man behind the door.

At the sound of the door slamming open, two things happened simultaneously. The seated man jumped up and spun his body to cover the rear of the plane, and Hanna shot him in the back of the head with a .22 caliber American Arms mini-revolver that she carried in her purse. As Tuck flew out of the toilet, the second man made the mistake of waiting to get a visual before aiming his weapon, and Tuck shot him twice in the face with the .380, dropping him instantly.

Now both Emily and Tuck Junior were crying which added to the confusion in the cabin. Amos had made a lunge for the cockpit when the toilet door flew open, and now both pilots were unconscious but still strapped in.

"Maggie, I need some help up here," he shouted back to the stunned Maggie O'Brien.

Maggie quickly got out of her seat and helped him drag the two pilots into the cabin.

"Look for something to tie them up with, Hon," Amos said to her sweetly, "I've got to fly this plane.

"I love a man with a sense of responsibility," she said sarcastically, "Hanna are you okay?"

Hanna just nodded as she slid the .22 back into her purse and cuddled the children.

"Gosh she looks so sweet and innocent, but she scares the hell out of me sometimes," Maggie thought as she took the men's belts and tied their hands behind them.

Tuck took the handguns from the two dead men and searched them for papers, but found nothing other than some official paperwork from Reggie Smythe. He came forward to Hanna and took Emily up in his arms.

"It's all right, Emily. Momma kept that bad man from hurting me," he reassured her. "Everything is all right now so climb back over there and go to sleep."

Emily gave him a hug and crawled back across her mother to get the nap that Tuck had told her to take.

"Where are we headed, Amos?" he asked as he moved to the cockpit.

"Right now, it would just be a guess, but I'd say that it was somewhere in South America. You need to wake one of the pilots up and get him to talk," Amos replied.

"Okay, I'll need you to get it down on the deck and cut our speed. I'm going to open the door," Tuck replied.

"Give me a minute or two," Amos told him.

Tuck made his way back to the pilots that were starting to move around a bit.

"I know that you guys are awake. Where were you taking us?" he asked.

The men just glared at him angrily.

"Have it your way, friends," Tuck just smiled coldly and moved to the hatch, "How much longer, Amos?" he shouted.

"About three minutes, Tuck. I'm trying not to disturb the other passengers," came the reply.

Maggie was looking at Tuck with a puzzled look on her face until he put his hand on the door release. A look of pure terror crossed her face as she realized what Michael Tucker was going to do.

"You heard him, men. You have three minutes before the door comes open and then I will need some answers to my question," he told the pilots who were now looking at him wild-eyed with fear.

Tuck turned and moved to drag the bodies, one at a time, to the door, and then waited for Amos.

"Okay, Tuck, you should be able to open it now," he shouted back.

Tuck pulled the door handle and let the door swing downward where it hung by the restraint cables. He grabbed the first dead man and pulled him to the door before pushing him out with his feet. The second followed in the same manner.

"Okay boys, which one wants to go first?" he reached down and took the collar of the co-pilot and started for the door with him.

"Wait, wait, I'll tell you what you want to know, just don't throw me out," the man started sobbing.

"Do you feel the same way?" Tuck asked the pilot.

"Yes sir, I have a family that wants me home," the man answered in relief.

"Start talking and make it convincing!" Tuck had a hardness to his voice.

Maggie seemed to breathe a sigh of relief and got up to move to the cockpit with Amos.

"Amos, he was going to throw those men out of the plane!" she whispered to her husband. Amos leaned over to her and replied, "He wasn't really, just wanted to scare them a bit. Keep your voice down."

The pilot told Tuck, "We were to drop you and your family off in LaCeiba, Honduras, and then return to Kinston."

"Was there a contact mentioned?" Tuck asked.

"Only that we taxi to cargo terminal C-3 and make the transfer," he replied with fear in his eyes.

"Is this true?" Tuck asked the co-pilot.

"Yes, except that I heard a name, Raul something like he might be the contact," the co-pilot stammered.

Tuck reached the door and got it retracted, "You men just make yourselves comfortable there while I make a phone call."

"O'Brien here." answered the hard voice on the other end.

"We've been waylaid by Amos' friend in Kingston. The situation is under control, but we are headed for Honduras and a meeting with a man named Raul in cargo hanger C-3. Do you know him?" Tuck asked.

"Well, that can only mean that Henry cracked and is probably dead. I would have thought that he could have held out longer. A team will be on the move as soon as I can get a call in, so hang tight for a few minutes," Shaun ended the call.

"Take her back up to altitude, Amos, but keep it slow. We need to give Shaun time to act," Tuck told Amos and then sat down with Hanna.

"Are you okay?" he asked quietly.

"A little shaky, but glad the kids are going to be safe," she responded as she leaned onto his shoulder.

"We will be able to relax when we get to Miami, Hon. Try to put this behind you as soon as possible, if you can," Tuck kissed her on the forehead and moved to the cockpit.

"As soon as we can turn this bird around, I want to go back and get the SeaStar," he told Amos.

"Are you crazy, Tuck? If we drop this back in that airport, Reggie will have us shot as we exit the plane," he replied, dumbfounded.

"Not if his pilot is the one doing the flying and talking. He can tell your friend Reggie that the operation was a success, and the packages were delivered," Tuck told him, "By the time he discovers the ruse, I will have him in duct tape, and you will have the SeaStar back."

"You know, that just might work. I saw the way the pilot warmed up to you back there...you know, just before you closed the door," Amos laughed.

"Well, that door can open right back up if need be," he replied with a grin, although there was no humor in it.

CHAPTER FOUR

Pastor Robert Pike sat behind the desk of his small office in the run down mission that he and his wife, Abigail, had taken charge of almost two years before. Now he was meeting with two of his parishioners to discuss an outreach in the very poor community when the secretary knocked and then opened the door.

"Excuse me Padre, but there is a man outside that says he needs to see you," she declared.

"Native or Anglo?" was his response.

"Big and black, but American," she answered.

"Give me a minute, and then send him in," Bob told her, "Luis, Jorge, we can continue this discussion tomorrow. Right now, I have to see this man."

Both men got up and left the room. Bob reached into the right-hand desk drawer, withdrew a 1911 Rock Island .45ACP, and worked the slide. With the heavy pistol cocked and locked, he placed it on the desk under his right hand and waited.

At six-feet-four-inches and two hundred and eighty pounds, the very muscular man in his forties was an impressive sight as he entered the room after a brief knock on the door, "Excuse me, Pastor Pike, but Shaun O'Brien sent me."

"Really? I haven't seen Mr. O'Brien in a few months. What does he need?" Bob replied, his hand tensing to pick up the .45, which didn't go unnoticed by his visitor.

"He said to tell you that 'The cougar is on the prowl', " came the response.

Bob relaxed at the mention of the pass phrase, "Have a seat and tell me what is going on."

"Thank you, sir. I got a call just a few minutes ago from Shaun and hurried over to make sure that the building here was secure. I also have a team at your residence, so if you would call your wife and tell her that we are friendlies, I would appreciate it," he answered.

Recognizing the urgency in the man's voice, Bob made the phone call immediately.

"Abigail, there are some men outside that are there to protect you," he told her.

"Protect me from what? What is going on, Bob?" Abigail sounded alarmed.

"I'll know in a few minutes. Stay calm, and stay inside," he told her and ended the call, "Okay, I'm with her, what is going on?"

"Your friend, Henry Albright, went missing early this morning in Washington State. Michael Tucker and his family have been taken along with Shaun's son-in-law and his wife, and they are on the way here. I am part of the team that is going to raid the hanger at the airport where we believe the man responsible is waiting on them to arrive," the stranger told him.

"Are the Tuckers all right? How did Shaun get wind of this? Are they after my wife and me?" A thousand questions ran through Bob's mind, but those were the only ones that became vocal.

"Tuck is fine. Apparently, he and his wife disabled the captors and took control of the plane. We don't know who all is going to be targeted, but hopefully, that information will be forth coming after the raid which should be going down even as we are talking," he told him.

"I didn't get your name," Bob said as he stood to shake the man's hand.

"My dad named me Raleigh, but my friends call me Hurricane," he answered with a big smile as the arm with triceps as big as a Smithfield ham extended to take Bob's hand.

"Thanks for coming, Hurricane. Now, what can I do to help our friends out?" Bob asked.

"Just wait here with me for now, Bob. Shaun will call when out men have secured the airport, and then we will go out there to see your friends on the plane," he told him.

Twenty minutes later, Hurricane's phone rang. He answered it and then handed it to Bob Pike, "It's Shaun."

"Hello, Shaun. can you tell me what is going on?" Bob asked.

"Hello, Bob. I'm not on the ground there, but one of my teams has apprehended a certain Raul Garza who we think is linked to the disappearance of Henry Albright a few hours ago. I'm certain that Hurricane has filled you in on that. The only unknown is whether or not you and Abigail are going to be affected. I don't think so, but you could be used for leverage to get close to the Tuckers," Shaun responded.

"I can see how that could happen. What do you need for Abby and I to do?" Bob asked.

"I have a safe house in Miami, Bob. I want you two to fly up with Hurricane and his team for a week or until we can get this sorted out," Shaun answered, "Now that is only a suggestion, understand, but I can provide protection up here that we can't down there."

"I understand, Shaun. I'll call Abby right now and tell her to pack a bag. When do we leave?" Bob asked.

"As soon as that bag is packed," Shaun told him and then ended the call.

"Well, Hurricane, I guess we are going on a trip," Bob said as he handed the phone back, "Give me a few minutes to call my wife and give a few orders to the secretary, then I'll be ready."

"I'll wait outside with my men, Sir," the big man got up and left the room.

Bob sat there for a few seconds before making his calls and wondered how all of this worked into God's plan for him and Abigail, a plan which had seemed so clear just a few brief hours before.

CHAPTER FIVE

Tuck's phone rang just as he was explaining the situation to the bound pilots. Rather, he was explaining their situation to them, and the dire straits that they now found themselves in.

"Go ahead, Shaun," he answered.

"Tuck, we've got him! Raul Garza, does that ring a bell?" Shaun asked.

"No, I don't think that we've run across that one. but we have sure stepped on enough toes that he might be a family member of one of them," Tuck answered.

"Well, you go get the SeaStar back, and make sure that Amos' friend, Reggie, feels your appreciation," Shaun told him.

"It will be a pleasure. I'll call as soon as we are airborne," Tuck replied.

"Fly straight into Miami. It looks like the cover is blown anyway. Tell Amos to dock it down by my boat. I'll have transportation standing by," Shaun ended the call.

"Okay, Amos, let's go back and surprise Mister Smythe," Tuck told him, "You guys need to put on your best faces now, and I don't want to hear the first word in Patois. Do you understand?"

"Completely, Sir. Now if you will just untie us, we'll get you all back to Kinston," the pilot told him.

"I'll untie you when we get close enough to hail Reggie and tell him the packages have been delivered as ordered," Tuck told him.

Both pilots seemed to sulk a bit but did not cause any trouble. The truth was they were not only shaken by the earlier events, but this was not what they had signed on with Reginald Smythe for.

Neither of them had any intention of doing anything that would keep them from getting home to their respective families, and even seem almost anxious to help.

Thirty minutes seemed to drag by before Amos called to Tuck, "I'm ready for our pilots now."

"Okay men. I'm going to untie you so that you can get the circulation back into your hands. Get on up there and get behind the controls. Just remember that I will be standing behind you at all times with a gun to your heads. At the first whisper of a problem, you won't be having any more. Do I make myself clear?" Tuck gave them their orders.

"Perfectly, Sir," they said simultaneously.

"Let's get it going then," he told them and ushered the pilots to the cockpit.

Twenty minutes later, they had made radio contact with the tower at Kingston and were on approach when a call came in from Reggie Smythe.

"Cessna alpha sierra bravo niner two zero come in," the radio crackled.

"Go ahead," the older pilot spoke into the mike.

"Has the package been delivered?" Reggie asked.

"The package was dropped off just as you requested, Sir," was the reply.

"Were there any problems?" Reggie asked.

The pilot turned to look at Tuck before answering.

"Tell him that there was a brief bit of gun play, and his men were taken to the hospital," Tuck coached him.

"I'm afraid that Rawlings and Murphy were injured by a bit of gunfire, Sir. They were taken to the hospital by the local authorities, and we decided to come on back," the pilot told him.

There as a brief silence before Reggie responded, "I'll meet you at the hanger."

"Roger, Sir."

"That was very good, men. Now, do we have to worry about running into a bunch of body guards at the hanger?" Tuck asked.

"Usually there are not, just mechanics," the co-pilot responded.

They were on final approach now, and Tuck moved back a bit so they could relax. Amos moved everyone to the rear of the cabin and out of direct line of sight while Maggie helped Hanna with the children. After a smooth touchdown, they taxied to the hanger that Reggie indicated, and there he was, radiant in his white suit and Panama hat, cocked just so. Tuck was looking forward to messing that image up just a little.

When the plane parked at the hanger entrance, the co-pilot dropped the door so that Reggie could enter. He came bounding up the steps without a care in the world. Just as he ducked his lanky form to clear the door, Tuck quickly wrapped a belt around his neck and slammed him face first into the seats opposite the entry.

"Amos, get everybody off of the plane, and keep an eye on these two," Tuck shouted as he tightened the noose around Reggie's neck.

"We won't be any trouble, Sir. I promise," the pilot said.

"Keep an eye on them anyway," Tuck repeated.

Hanna had Emily on her shoulder so that she wouldn't see Tuck choking the daylights out of Mister Smythe.

"Is Daddy hurting that man, Momma?" Tuck heard as they squeezed past him.

"Just having a little talk with him, Dear. We'll just let them finish their business," Hanna responded as they left the plane.

Maggie followed with Junior. Amos stopped for a second, "Don't be too long, Partner. We've got a plane to liberate."

"I'll be right behind you. Just get us some transportation to the plane," Tuck answered, "Now Reggie, you and I are going to come to an understanding."

Five minutes later, Tuck emerged from the Cessna and trotted to where Amos was standing with the group, "Well, where is the boat?"

"Don't need one. Look inside," Amos pointed to the SeaStar which was sitting in the hanger, fueled and ready.

"Well, go get her ready to roll. I'll wait here with our new friends until you taxi her out," he said.

Amos led the others inside and loaded them aboard the SeaStar without attracting too much attention. He shortened the checklist considerably, checking only that they had fuel, before firing up the turboprop and bringing it to a slow taxi to the door.

As they waited nervously for the sea plane to clear the door, the two pilots turned to Tuck, "We don't have a job now, and not many prospects. Will you tell your boss that we would like to work for him?"

"Guys, you really don't know what you are asking, but I will tell him. Look, for what it's worth, I'm sorry about roughing you up...just part of my job," Tuck told them.

"We understand. It was an invigorating experience...like being in a cowboy movie," the young one told him with a smile.

"Well, good luck to you. I've got a ride to catch," Tuck said and walked to the plane which had cleared the hanger door.

Amos got the hatch open and Tuck ducked under the wing and climbed into the cabin.

"Hold onto something everybody, we are going to full throttle," Amos called out as the seven hundred and twenty-four horsepower turboprop roared to maximum throttle.

The radio started squawking immediately as they raced into sight of the tower, but the SeaStar was wheels up in less than five hundred feet and effortlessly climbing for the maximum ceiling of thirty thousand plus feet. Amos held it open until they passed twenty thousand feet before leveling off a bit and easing back the throttle with the airspeed at three hundred knots.

"Good work, Amos," Tuck told him with a grin.

"Well, did you kill Reggie?" Amos asked.

"No, but he will be sore for a few days. I locked him in the toilet before I said my goodbyes and got my Krugerrand back," Tuck answered.

"Well, go on back and hug your wife. We'll be in Miami in a couple of hours so I've got to get on the horn to get our flight cleared across Cuba and points North," Amos told him.

Tuck slid into a seat beside Hanna and Emily got in his lap, "Almost home now, Love."

"Well, we might be almost out of danger, but we are a long way from home, Michael," Hanna said as she lay her head on his free shoulder.

"Someday soon, though, Hanna, someday soon," Tuck told her.

"From your lips to God's ears," she replied, "Maggie, did you ever just want a home that you could relax in?"

"I think that I did one time, Hanna, but so much has gone on in my life since we were in school, that I never give it a thought anymore. Well, I never did give it a thought until I held Emily and now Tuck Junior," she smiled.

"That's Bubba to his friends, Maggie," Tuck laughed.

"Over my dead body," Hanna chimed in.

"Well, when Uncle Amos and I take him fishing then," Tuck conceded.

The rest of the flight was one filled with the joyful banter of a group of friends that belied the stress of the past few hours, and soon they were descending on Miami and the dock where Shaun kept his boat.

As Amos taxied slowly to the dock where they were keeping the company boat and seaplane, Tuck surveyed the area with a pair of Leupold binoculars. As they made a turn around the stern of a large cruise liner, he noticed two men standing on the dock in the space where they were going to moor the plane.

"Looks like we have a welcoming committee, Amos," Tuck said.

"Is it safe?" Hanna questioned from behind him.

"That's questionable," he answered with a laugh, "It's Mike and Jerry."

"Uncle Jerry, Uncle Jerry!" Emily brightened up, moving to look out the window.

"Uncle Mike too, Dear," Hanna told her.

Amos killed the motor as the big man they called Mike got hold of the wing and maneuvered the boat to the slip.

Tuck opened the cabin door, "Hey guys, who did you hack off to get this good duty?"

Jerry came to the plane and took Emily from Hanna, "Hello, Emily. How is my favorite girl today?"

"My name is Rebecca, but you can call me Becca, Uncle Jerry," she told him sternly.

"Uh, okay Becca. How about a big hug?" he replied.

"Save one for me too, Becca!" Mike chimed in.

"How are things looking Mike?" Tuck asked him.

"I've got two men up on the roadway watching us and any incoming traffic. It's clear now, but we shouldn't linger out here any longer than necessary," Mike replied.

"Let's get going then," Tuck responded loudly enough for the rest to hear him, and they headed up the pier to the waiting vehicles with Tuck carrying his namesake.

The ride through Miami Beach to the nondescript industrial neighborhood where the safe house was located took almost forty-five minutes in moderate traffic. Tuck and Hanna both surveyed every passing car suspiciously out of habit, even though the SUV that they were riding in was heavily armored and carried official government plates.

They arrived at an old building that looked deserted at first glance, but a careful study of the top floors would have revealed modern glazing meant to be not only solar efficient, but also bulletproof, and there were security cameras mounted at the upper corners of the brickwork.

The heavy metal roll up door opened surprisingly fast when they turned off the street and closed equally fast once the two vehicles were inside. The first made a sweeping turn that allowed the one that Mike was driving to pull up to within a few feet of an elevator. Tuck noticed that there were several others in the garage, two of which also wore government plates.

"Okay guys," Mike announced, "let's get out of here and upstairs. Jerry and I will keep this area clean."

"Thanks, Mike. If anything heats up, give me a call immediately," Tuck shook his hand.

"Will do, Boss, but it is going to be quiet for a while. You folks go relax," he replied.

CHAPTER SIX

In the old fishing trawler's hold, a rough sanitary room had been hastily fashioned with sheets of five mil plastic hung from the overhead on lengths of PVC pipe rigged for the occasion. In front of the room was a desk with what looked to be a game computer hooked to a thirty-two-inch monitor, one side of which was displaying the vitals of a very large man that was strapped to a hospital bed in the middle of the room. Directly over him was a high-intensity light normally used in an operating room, and to his right was an I.V. stand with bags of clear fluids that were being fed into his arm through tubes that terminated in the veins of his bruised forearm. His chest heaved slightly as the man struggled to breathe, and the only other sign of life was the chirping of the monitor that was connected to his body in several places.

Sitting at the desk and observing the monitor was a slender built man in his fifties with a hard look to his features, and in a chair next to him but facing the man on the bed was a heavy set man with the look of an over the hill prize fighter, complete with bent nose, cauliflowered ear, and thick set eyebrows growing haphazardly from ridges made up of mostly scar tissue.

"In the old days, I could have gotten the information that Julius needs from this pig in a few hours," the big man mumbled.

"Alas, Yuri, these are not the old days, and Julius doesn't want any marks on the body when we dump him," the slender man replied, "Why don't you go see what they are cooking tonight while I finish up down here. I'll meet you in the galley."

"Julius wants a constant guard on him, Otto," the one called Yuri nodded toward the bed.

"That one has enough sodium thiopental in his system to keep a horse under for several days. He is not going anywhere!" Otto answered brusquely, "Besides, where would he go?"

Both men headed for the gangway that led to the upper decks and the galley, leaving the comatose prisoner alone in the cold, plastic enclosed space with only the sound of bilge water sloshing beneath the rusting deck plates and the muffled thumping of the diesel engine to keep him company. Unnoticed by his captors in the glare of the operating room lighting was the hand that had slowly trapped the I.V. tube and crushed it against the bed frame, slowing the flow of sodium thiopental into the big man's body.

The minutes passed slowly as Henry Albright struggled to stay conscious so that he could choke off the flow of barbiturates into his body. He was surprised to have regained enough consciousness to be able to assess his situation, but the mention of sodium thiopental explained why he had. On a body as large as his, sodium thiopental wore off more quickly than it would have on a younger, leaner man.

"And to think the doctors have been after me to lose weight," he laughed to himself, "Even I know that Propofol would have been the drug of choice to keep a fat old war horse down."

He lay there quietly waiting for an opportunity to capitalize on his good fortune, even though he still had arm and leg restraints on. Finally, almost an hour later, he heard the men returning to check on him. His eyes darted quickly to a table next to his right side, and the array of syringes laid out on it, and a plan started forming in his drug-soaked mind.

"You see, Yuri, our guest is still right where we left him. You worry for nothing, my friend," Otto joked.

"Perhaps, but you can never be too careful with one like that, Otto," Yuri replied as he moved to inspect Henry's restraints.

"Yuri, I left my glasses in the galley. Keep an eye on him and make sure he doesn't get away," Otto laughed as he turned to the door.

Yuri moved to Henry's left side away from the I.V. stand and inspected the Velcro strap that held his wrist to the bed.

"Ah my friend, you thought that Yuri would not see that this strap needs tightening, eh?" He said to the man in the bed.

Yuri reached for the Velcro and pulled it loose so that he could tighten it against Henry's arm, and in the split second that the restraint was unfastened, Henry jerked his arm free and reached across his body for the one syringe that he had spotted earlier. Even in his drugged consciousness, he knew that a needle that long was made to reach the heart muscle through the chest wall. In a fraction of a second, it was firmly implanted in Yuri's chest, and those massive, fight scarred hands grasping Henry's wrist could not stop him from delivering a lethal dose of digitalis into Yuri's heart muscle, which stopped immediately.

Henry started to work immediately to loosen the other straps and get himself off the table before Otto returned. He just made it to the hatch on his shaky legs when Otto came through and walked right past him. Another syringe loaded with air found its way into Otto's carotid artery, and he died without a sound as a bubble found his brain.

Henry moved slowly back to Yuri and began stripping the man of his clothes. Except for the pants being a bit short, Yuri had the same build, and Henry needed clothes. Once he had dressed, he pried up a deck plate and slid both bodies into the oily water that swirled in the bilges. Even if they were there for a week, the fish smell would mask the odor of decomposition.

After dumping the two men, Henry moved to the computer and made a quick check for an internet service. He noted the IP address of his station and hastily got an email to Shaun to track that IP, setting up a continuous ping of Google. Hanging by the hatch were two heavy weather jackets with fur lined hoods, so he grabbed the largest one and put it on. To his surprise, he came upon a small Beretta .32 in the right-hand pocket, and a quick check proved it was loaded.

Henry staggered slightly as he moved into a dimly lit companionway that ran the width of the ship just outside of the hatch and moved quickly to the ladder that led topside; away from the stench of the space that he had just left. As he stepped carefully through the hatch, stopping to check for any sign of life, he noticed that except for an occasional bump, the vessel was not rocking or pitching like it had been. This could only mean that they had docked somewhere, and Henry's time before discovery was getting shorter by the minute.

CHAPTER SEVEN

"Tuck," was all that he said when the burner rang.

"Well, I got an email from Henry. He is on a ship somewhere, apparently, but he must have gotten the computer mixed up with a phone. I need a GPS signal for a position, and that computer is buried in a VPN. I'm still in Washington waiting, but right now, it is a dead end," Shaun reported, "Has Hurricane arrived with our other guests yet?"

"At least Henry is still alive or was when the email was sent. The big guy isn't here yet but should be in any minute. Mike and Jerry are with the security team downstairs so they'll let us know. Should we put the crew on standby?" Tuck answered.

"I think that might be prudent, Tuck. If we get a lead close to Miami, we will need a quick response. I've got Henry's people out here if we need them, and they are pretty agitated," Shaun told him.

"I'll pass the good news onto Hanna, and get everything ready. If you need me to, I can catch the red eye out and be there by morning," Tuck told him.

"Which might be just what whoever is behind this wants. No, stay there with your team and keep an eye on the family. When this breaks, we will all be busier than we want to be, so rest up. I'll call as soon as I hear something else," Shaun ended the call.

"Did you get all of that, Hon?" Tuck asked as Hanna walked up behind him.

"I heard you say that Uncle Henry is alive. Is there anything else?" Hanna asked softly.

"No, just that we are on standby for a bit, kind of like a vacation," Tuck smiled as he spoke.

"Some vacation. I can't even go shopping!" Hanna pretended to pout.

"When this is over, I'll take you to New York for some real shopping," Tuck responded.

"When this is over, I want to see Kathryn. She needs to see these grandkids," Hanna told him.

"Well, Kathryn first and then New York," he gave her a hug.

"You've got yourself a date, Big Boy," she replied as they both laughed, "Now go get everything ready so we can find Uncle Henry!"

Henry stood by the open hatch that led to the open deck and listened for the sounds that would indicate where they might be, but there was only silence, except for the occasional laugh and some loud talking forward of his position. The air was crisp and cold, not Washington weather to be sure, but hardly Arctic either. After the area where he had been tied up in, is was refreshing to feel the cold on his skin and in his nose. He took one look out of the hatchway to make certain that he was alone on this section of the ship and then stepped out into the fading daylight. Taking hold of the rail with his left hand, Henry slowly made his was toward the gangway that he could see about fifty feet further up, being careful to keep his hat and hood pulled low over his face. Just a few more steps and he would be off the ship, but where that was he could only guess.

"Hey, Yuri! Yuri!" a loud voice rang out from above, "Are we playing cards again tonight?"

Henry froze momentarily and then raised his right hand to briefly wave, but did not look back. Two more steps and he was on the gangway. He made his way to the end as quickly as he could without giving away the fact that he'd recently been drugged, and had almost no muscle control. The end of the gangway was behind him at last, so Henry stopped briefly before starting down the fifty-yard long dock toward a decrepit fish house that looked as if it had seen many winters. As he walked, every nerve in his body seemed to be anticipating the arrival of whoever it was that had him kidnapped. Henry surveyed the area surrounding the fish house and saw no homes or anything else that would indicate this was a lively community, and right now he needed to find someone with a cell phone or an automobile if he was going to make his escape.

In the distance he could make out tall pines and not much else, although a small service sized road ran off to his right as he neared the building. Even though the drug was rapidly wearing off, he didn't want to chance an encounter with anyone, so Henry made his way carefully around to the back of the fish house and looked for a way in. As he slowly opened a weathered door, the sound of laughter and loud talking came from inside. He listened for a minute to the language which was in English, albeit not very well spoken. From the accents, he deduced that most of the men were native fishermen, although there was one clear voice that stood out among them. Something about that made the hair on his neck stand up. Henry pulled the door quietly shut and looked around behind him. There was an old shack standing about a hundred yards away in the edge of a tall pine forest with plenty of cover to hide him as he made his way carefully over and peeked in a dirty window.

From what little he could see, the cabin was empty, but there was a duffel on the kitchen table. Henry made it to the rear door and pushed it open slowly. He looked for any type of phone, or a set of keys, but found nothing. The duffel was another story. Inside was fifty thousand dollars in small bills, a Glock 20 10mm, and his picture. Figuring that the contractor was inside the main building and would soon know that his prey had flown the coop, Henry decided that there was no time to waste as he grabbed the bag and made it out through the back door, stopping only to grab a piece of an old tarp, a box of strike-on-any-surface matches that were sitting on a shelf by the small wood stove, and an old lantern that had about half of a tank of kerosene. Now to find out just where he was.

Henry ducked his big frame quickly into the forest that seemed to surround the cabin and fish house. The cover of the wooded area would help cover his track in the growing twilight, but he was concerned about freezing to death before morning when he was certain that whoever had been hired to kill him would find an easy target.

"The hell with that," thought Henry to himself, "If I'm going to get killed, I'll make this guy work for his money!"

He walked slowly through the brushy undergrowth toward the dock area until he came to what looked like a service road that ran westerly toward some house lights about a mile away. Since he had not seen any transportation in this area, Henry decided to try and walk the road close to the tree line and take his chances with someone from the settlement being able to get him to safety.

Just as he started to step out from the tree line, a group of men came laughing from the direction of the fish house and headed toward the boat. Henry pulled the Glock from the bag along with an extra magazine which he had dropped into the jacket pocket with the small Beretta and then waited for them to board the boat. He would only have a few minutes to cover about two hundred yards of clear area and get in the woods on the other side before they came back looking for him, of this his muddled brain was certain. Twenty years ago this would not have been a problem, but twenty years ago, Henry didn't weigh two-hundred and eighty pounds soaking wet. As soon as the last man went into the side hatch, Henry took off at a tottering run for the cover of the shoreline woods. His heart was pounding from the excitement and exertion, but living in the mountainous region of Washington State as he did had left him in better shape than he had hoped for. His large frame had just cleared the tree line on the opposite side of the road when it sounded like all hell had broken out on the ship. He knew that now was not the time to look back, but tried to set an even pace through the dark woods and brush tangles to put some distance between himself and the man that had been hired to kill him.

CHAPTER EIGHT

Bob and Abigail Pike arrived at the expansive safe house about two hours after Tuck and Hanna, marveling at how the thousands of square feet of the abandoned plant upper floors had been turned into several luxury apartments with recreational space complete with a heated pool.

"Man, Tuck, I'd have been here sooner if we had known about this setup," Bob said with a grin.

"Well, we probably would have preferred to stay on the island, but for safety's sake, this is certainly a better choice. Who did you come in with?" Tuck replied.

"Some big fellow named Hurricane," Bob told him, "He is downstairs with the others. What do you know about Henry anyway? Has Shaun found out anything?" Bob replied.

"Nothing yet, although there was an email that they couldn't trace. I'm waiting on word now," he answered, "Why don't we show you and Abigail to your rooms and then we'll get something to eat."

Hanna and Abigail had already walked to the recreation area with Emily so she could ride her tricycle around the bare floor, Tuck and Bob caught up with them there.

"Well, what are your plans for when this settles down?" Abigail asked both Tuck and Hanna.

"I would like to see Kathryn again," Hanna told her, "Other than that, we haven't really made any."

"You know that the family would be welcome to stay with us. Who knows, Honduras might grow on you," Bob laughed.

Tuck's cell phone buzzed, "Sorry guys, it's Shaun."

Tuck moved to a corner of the large room and took the call. There was not a word spoken as Hanna listened for any word of her uncle. Tuck ended the call and came back to the group.

"Well, what did Shaun say?" Hanna asked impatiently.

"He says for me to put a team together and get to Seattle as fast as we can. Shaun didn't elaborate so I'm thinking that he has an idea who has Henry and needs a team to grab him," Tuck replied, "I've got to go now, Hon. Can you pack me a bag while I get the men ready?"

"Of course, Michael, but don't you want me to come along?" Hanna asked.

"Just the team on this one, Love. Stay put until you hear from me. Remember, we have a shopping trip in New York City when this is over," Tuck gave her a big hug and then turned his attention to the kids before leaving the room.

"Sometimes I just want to shoot something!" Hanna said quietly to his retreating back.

Bob and Abigail just exchanged concerned glances.

"Hanna, have you had any sleep?" Abigail asked.

"Not much, no. I'm expressing milk every three hours, and trying to nap between feedings," she replied, "That's not been working so well lately."

"Bob and I will take care of the children while you get rested. Where is his bag?" Abigail said gently, "No arguments now, little Tuck needs his momma to be one hundred percent."

"Abigail, you are amazing!" Hanna gave her a hug before dashing off then, over her shoulder, "His milk is in the fridge."

"Well played, Honey," Bob told her as Hanna disappeared from the recreation area, "I'll take over with Emily while you take the baby. You're so much better with diapers, as I recall."

Abigail gave him a peck on the cheek and picked up the day seat that Tuck Junior was sleeping in.

"You men," she laughed, "Ready to conquer the world but afraid of a little poop!"

Bob just laughed and walked across the expanse of the room to sit on a training bench while he kept an eye on Emily. Tuck came back in about that time and looked surprised.

"Where is everybody?" he asked.

"Hanna is going to sleep for a while, and Abigail is watching Junior," Bob responded, "When you get back, we need to talk about Hanna."

"What's going on, Bob?" Tuck asked.

"Hanna is showing signs of extreme stress, Tuck. Coupled with her post-partum hormones, it could be extremely difficult for her to cope with all of this action. You need to think about retiring for a bit and getting her some counseling," Bob said as sincerely as he could.

Tuck just looked at him for a few seconds before nodding his head in agreement.

"I've been worried about her since the baby came. She cries a lot when she doesn't think I can hear. Now, this mess with Henry has driven us out of our home," Tuck answered, "Look, Bob, the men are waiting for me, and I have to go. Can you and Abigail help while you're here?"

"We'll do what we can, Tuck, but when you get back, you need to think about getting her into counseling...the kind you probably should have had when we first met," Bob shook his hand, "Be safe, boy, and get back as soon as possible."

"Daddy, Daddy, watch me!" Emily rode her tricycle toward them as fast as she could, and then slid it sideways on the slick floor with a huge squeal of delight.

"Come here, Pumpkin. Give Daddy a hug," Tuck picked her up from the tricycle, "Uncle Jerry and I are going to see Uncle Shaun. What do you want me to bring you back?"

"I want a pony!" Emily exclaimed.

"We'll have to check with Momma when I get back, Sugar. You take care of her and your brother now," Tuck hugged her and set her back on the toy.

Bob noticed the wetness in his eyes and looked the other way for a few seconds. When he looked back, Tuck was already at the door and Emily was asking for a push. He gave her a big smile and thought of how mysterious were God's ways as he scooted the little angel across the gym floor. One minute they were in a declining ministry, and the next they were ministering to a family that they had mourned as dead just a short time before, now suddenly very much alive and in need of comfort that only could come from above.

Tuck didn't let the things that he was feeling distract him from the mission at hand. His team this trip would be comprised of Jerry and Mike, both ex-special forces, and Raleigh, a highly skilled weapons expert, both projectile and blade. Amos would be their pilot, but only after they congregated in Kansas City. Their gear would be waiting in Washington at a pre-arranged location that Shaun would disclose after they were on the Beechcraft King Air. The other men would keep an eye on the fortress of a safe house until they returned. No thought was given to any other alternative.

CHAPTER NINE

With darkness almost total, and the sub-freezing night air making anything other than shivering difficult, Henry waited until the voices had moved along the road toward what appeared to be a village before crossing over into the forest on the other side. He made about one hundred yards into the dark woods before coming to a thick growth of young Sitka spruce that blocked his path. His brain was still suffering from the effects of the drug that had been administered, but Henry had a lifetime of woods lore beneath his belt, and almost instinctively, he put that to use in the hope of not freezing to death before dawn.

Working quickly in the half light, he bent three of the young trees together to form a small tent above him and tied them at the top with the belt that was holding up the pants previously belonging to the unfortunate Yuri. He quickly stripped the small underside branches from the trees and made a hut of sorts with the branches covering the wet ground. Once that was finished, Henry crawled inside and pulled the tarp around his shoulders. Fortunately, the old canvas was large enough to cover his body down to his feet, and also block the light from the lantern that Henry now placed between his legs and lit. Soon the heat was rising up to the opening near his neck along with the smell of kerosene smoke, but he knew that would be a small price to pay for being able to walk out of here in the morning.

Worn out from his exertion, with a waterproof tarp over his body and a dry mat of spruce bough under his rear, Henry lay back against the spruce and fell asleep until the heat of the lantern woke him briefly. The soft spattering of ice falling didn't keep him from nodding back off almost instantly after turning the wick of the lantern down, and the smell of the freshly broken Sitka spruce boughs let him know that he was still south of Alaska. In the distance, the sound of a wolf pack running came to him, but he was too exhausted to care about the danger they presented.

The cold early morning light was just making things visible in the thicket when Henry woke suddenly to something heavy lying on his feet. His hand gripped the Glock and slowly brought it up even as his eyes opened slowly to see what had crawled in with him during the night. As his eyes adjusted to the dim light, he was able to make out the shape of an older Malamute curled up, but looking as if he was keeping watch.

"Hello, old fellow," Henry spoke in a low voice, "When did you come in?"

The dog looked up at him but didn't move. Henry was surprised at how much clearer his mind was after sleeping almost all night in the small, makeshift shelter. His body didn't share the same rejuvenation, unfortunately, and he had trouble getting out and stretching. The dog came out with him wagging his plume of a tail but didn't leave his side.

"Homeless are you?" Henry took the chance to slowly reach down and scratch the animal behind the ear, "I'll tell you what, help me get out of here, and I'll do what I can for you...deal?"

It was then that he noticed the bloodied ear and a few places on the dog that suggested a fight. He retrieved his belt from the spruce tops, shaking a bit of ice onto him and the dog, and then picked up the money bag and the tarp. The lantern was out of fuel so Henry jettisoned it in hope of not needing it any longer.

The forest was quiet at this early hour, and the temperature seemed to be in the single digits. He would have to move to stay warm, and hopefully, find someone that could help him get to safety before his would-be killer could locate his whereabouts. Henry set off slowly through the woods in the general direction of the settlement whose lights he had seen the evening before. It paralleled the road for as long as they could.

The Malamute alerted Henry to possible danger before he had seen anything. He was watching the ground in front of him when the dog's hackles stood up and a slight rumble started in his throat. Henry dropped to one knee and strained to see or hear anything in front of them. After a minute, he could make out the sound of two people talking, but it sounded like they were about a hundred yards away through some dense cover. He reached over and patted the dog on the head.

"Okay fella, let's go see who is over there," Henry said in a low tone.

He checked the 10mm and the Beretta to make certain they both had a round in the chamber, then started a very slow stalk of the individuals on the other side of the tree line. The Malamute looked at him as if waiting for a command before moving out slightly ahead of Henry with his nose in the air. Henry continued moving ahead with one eye on the dog until they got to a brush cover where he could see the two men talking.

A taller, greasy looking man seemed to be berating another shorter man that was unmistakably Indian, "You're getting paid to find this guy, now have you seen anyone this morning or not?"

The Indian replied, "There hasn't been anyone that looks like the man that I'm supposed to be watching for by here since last night. My cousins up the road would have called me if he made it that far. Where is he going to go anyway? In case you haven't noticed, Bull Harbor is on an island!"

"Well, just keep looking for him to come by, the boss is furious that we let him get off the boat," the greasy man told him and walked off toward the fishing shack.

Henry watched him leave and then turned his attention to the Indian as he mounted a four-wheeler and rode off in the other direction.

"Come on, fella," he called to the dog softly, "we need to scout this place out while that guy is gone."

In the back of the house was a rack where the man had been drying salmon. A small fire still smoked below the large fish slabs that had been draped over the rack directly above to keep the insects away, although the cold had taken care of that duty so far. Henry took two of the largest pieces down and moved toward the house. There didn't seem to be anyone home so he eased in the back door after telling his new companion to wait, and giving him a portion of one of the fish.

Inside, the smell of wood smoke, stale beer, and bad hygiene hung heavy in the air so he moved quickly through the three room cabin to try and find a cell phone, to no avail. What he did find was an old Remington 700 chambered for the venerable 30-06 round and a box of ammo, which he hurriedly slung over his shoulder and made his way back out of the house, but not before picking up a large kitchen knife from the dirty table.

"Let's head for the woods, fella," he spoke to the dog, " I have a feeling somebody will be looking for this rifle real soon."

He knew after hearing the men talk that there were others in the settlement being paid to watch for him, so he moved directly away from the house and into the woods behind it. The news about this being an island and the settlement being named Bull Harbor told him exactly where he was, and also told him just how difficult it was going to be to get off of it. Hope Island, as this was called, had made the news with an innovative plan by the locals to farm salmon much like the one that he was now stripping the meat from with his teeth. He also knew that there was a small airport somewhere on the island, but didn't have a clue how to find it. The only planes that he had seen were two small pontoon equipped planes in the harbor area. Henry needed to find somebody with a cell phone, and he needed to find them quickly. It was just a fluke that he hadn't been found last night, and he knew his luck would not hold out much longer.

CHAPTER TEN

"All I know for certain is that the man we picked up in Honduras, Raul Silva, is a well known international bounty hunter. He was after a one-point-five-million dollar bounty on Henry's head. How he got the info on Tuck and his family, we couldn't get out of him," Shaun said to the man sitting across the table from him.

"That doesn't give us much to go on, Shaun. Perhaps if we could talk to this Raul gentleman he might shed a bit more light on the situation," came the reply.

Shaun was talking to one of Henry's trusted contacts in an intelligence community that seemed to be increasingly wary of giving him any information the further down Henry's list that he went. This one was a man that he had met in Texas during the trouble that the philandering FBI senior agent had caused, and Walter Grooms had been instrumental in helping Henry fake their demise.

"Well, there is a problem with that, Walter. You see, one of the men that conducted the raid in Honduras and delivered Silva to us got a little carried away during the interrogation process. Silva did not survive," Shaun told him.

"Ah, those hot-blooded Latinos. We certainly had a few of those back in Texas, didn't we, Shaun?" Grooms replied, leaning back in his chair with his hands folded behind his head.

"Walter, I understand that the FBI may be reluctant to get involved, but most of my men look to Henry as a father figure of sorts. He certainly takes care of his own in that regard," Shaun replied.

"Okay then, that doesn't leave us much to go on, except the obvious facts that Henry Albright is missing, and we know that he didn't leave the country by plane, train, or automobile according to the several dozen agents that are in the chase. That leaves us with a ship, but nothing that has been within small boat range of our coast has any sign of him onboard, and believe me, the Coast Guard has boarded every one of them. I'm thinking a private fishing vessel, possibly an older trawler or something like it. We've contacted all of the big commercial names up the coast, but they are clean also. We've also done some satellite scans of the area all of the way north of Vancouver Island for vessel traffic, but there has been a heavy cloud cover over the coast for the past week with has blinded us pretty effectively," Grooms told him.

"I've got a team in transit if we can get a general area to search, Walter. What is the weather looking like?" Shaun asked.

"We've been told that it will be a week before this system moves through and probably a two-day window after that. If I were you, I would land a team up past Vancouver and start looking from there North. I can't get boots on the ground without pissing off the Canadians, but you can. It would be worth a look," he replied.

"Well, it is better to be doing something than nothing, I suppose. It sure is frustrating to have all of this technology and not be able to find anything. I'll keep in touch by secure phone," Shaun said as he shook Agent Grooms' hand and left the room.

The next call was to Tuck as soon as he was clear of the FBI building in Seattle.

"Hey, Tuck, what's your twenty?" Shaun asked when Tuck answered his phone.

"Just leaving Kansas City, any word on Henry?" Tuck replied.

"No, but there has been a change in plans. Tell Amos to fly to Vancouver Island and set down just north of Ladysmith at the Nanaimo Airport. We'll rendezvous in Nanaimo," Shaun told him.

"Roger that, Chief. I'll relay that to Amos, and we'll see you up there," Tuck replied before ending the call.

"Relay what to me, Tuck?" Amos asked.

"We are headed for Canada, my friend, Vancouver Island to be a bit more specific and a city named Nanaimo," Tuck told him before leaning back in his seat and closing his eyes.

Abigail came into the living room to find Emily and Bob asleep in a recliner with the seventy-inch television playing a children's movie. She had Michael Junior in her arms with a bottle in his mouth. Hanna was still asleep in one of the six large bedrooms that were on this floor of the old building, and Abigail didn't want to wake her until it was time for her to express her milk.

As she walked slowly past Bob to another recliner, he opened one eye and smiled, "Been a while, hasn't it?" he asked softly.

"I never thought that I would have the chance to hold one this small, Bob. He smells so nice," Abigail had tears in her eyes.

"Until the diaper gets full anyway," he chuckled, "Emily wore me out."

"I think we know now why the good Lord brought us here. Hanna needs us, and these children need a little peace surrounding them," Abigail said in a low voice.

"Hanna needs some major counseling all right, but unless their lives get back to normal, all of the counseling in the world isn't going to help her," he replied.

"I know. Maybe we can just start by helping reduce her stress load, and maybe have a small bible study when the kids are down," Abigail suggested.

"Well, as long as it comes naturally, Dear. Pushing that on her right now might also push her away from us. Let's just take as much of the workload off until she gets acclimated to this place," Bob cautioned.

"Do you think that they will find Henry Albright?" she asked.

"If anyone can do it, Shaun's crew can, but it may be that he is already dead. Those guys run in some rough circles," he told her, "Just pray for Henry to come through this because his family needs him."

Hanna came into the room as they were talking looking like she had been run over.

"Hey, Hanna. Did you get some sleep?" Bob asked.

"Almost two hours, which is good for me. You don't know how much I appreciate you guys helping," she told them.

"We love you and the children, Hanna. Whatever we can do to help you while we are here, we want to do," Abigail responded.

"Just feeding Michael is a big help. Can you keep him for a little while longer? I have a date with my breast pump," she laughed.

"Of course we can. It's good to hear you laugh," Bob told her, "We haven't had any word from Tuck yet, but he said it might be late tonight before he could call."

"He'll be okay, I just hope they find Henry and get everything straightened out soon. We've had enough of hiding like animals in a hole, although this is a pretty swanky hole...as holes go," she laughed at the thought as she left the room.

"Well, what do you think?" Bob asked Abigail.

"I think that being here with us is the right medicine for Hanna. Once she is able to go back to her old lifestyle, she can put the past few years behind her," she answered, "Until then, we just need to make sure that she gets plenty of rest for the next few days, anyway."

"I agree, but I wonder if Miss Emily here is going to let me get some rest," he answered with a smile.

Emily just snuggled in closer to Bob.

CHAPTER ELEVEN

The two-hundred and fifty-foot trawler 'Midnight Sun' that was moored to the utility dock in Bull Harbor had been a spectacular vessel in her day, a day which had passed more than twenty years before. Now she had massive streaks of rust on her sides, and some of her superstructure was no longer deemed safe by Coast Guard regulations for the fishery that she had faithfully worked for so many years. The crew, made up largely from the local Native Indian population, was now feverishly trying to clean the rust bucket up before a scheduled Coast Guard inspection later that morning.

Working just as feverishly were six men who now had blocked all access to the lower hold where Henry Albright had been held. In a matter of less than an hour, all evidence that this area of the ship had been used for anything but fish preparation had disappeared. As the men left the Midnight Sun with several large boxes of equipment from the hold, the Coast Guard contingent arrived to start the inspection. The first thirty minutes were focused on the vessel's paperwork, which was in order, and then the inspectors poured over the vessel itself writing several pages of actionable violations of the code that would have to be addressed before she would work again.

The last place that they looked was in the two hold areas of the ship, one forward that had recently held several hundred boxes of fish, and then to the aft hold to finish the inspection.

"I'd like to take a look in the bilges," Petty Officer third class Matt Burgess told the seaman that accompanied him.

"Geez, Matt, can't we just let this one go? She isn't going to pass inspection anyway," Seaman Roy Chance asked.

"No, we need to make certain that she is seaworthy or not and that includes looking under those deck plates," Burgess told him, indicating the rusted diamond plate steel that covered the fish hold bilges.

Seaman Chance just shrugged his shoulders and motioned to the two Native crew members that were with them to get the plates up.

"HOLY CRAP!" one of the crew shouted when the second plate had been slid back to expose the bilge closer to the keel section. There in the oily black water were the bodies of two men, unrecognizable in the oily slop sloshing through the bilges.

"I need everyone to clear this area immediately," ordered Burgess, "Chance, make your way forward on the double and have the Lieutenant get down here. Somebody will have to call the authorities."

Seaman Chance and the crewmembers left the hold at a run with Chance holding his hand over his mouth to keep the vomit in until he was topside.

"Now there is something you don't see every day," Agent Walter Grooms said as he was half-heartedly scanning reports of emergency calls from as far away as Anchorage, Alaska in hopes of missing something extraordinary that might give them a lead on the whereabouts of Henry Albright.

"Get the Coast Guard Commandant for that area on the phone, and tell him that we need to be kept up to date on that story out of

Bull Harbor," Walter angrily ordered one of his people, and get me, Shaun O'Brien, also."

Agent Grooms went into his office to receive the calls and waited for the next one. There was a sense in his mind that this was somehow connected to Henry, who it was said had a particularly brutal side to his nature. Well, killing two men and sliding their bodies into a ship's bilge would certainly qualify for brutality, especially if they weren't dead when they went in. His thoughts were interrupted by his cell phone ringing.

"Agent Grooms here," he answered, "Yes Shaun, I've got something for you about two hundred miles north of Nanaimo. They found two bodies in the bilge of an old trawler that was being inspected in Bull Harbor."

"That's a lead, at least. We'll grab a float plane and head out as soon as the team is here," Shaun replied.

"Listen, Shaun, I have seen you in operation, so a word of warning. Please do not bring a bad light on the department up there. We still have to have a working relationship with the Canadians," Grooms implored him.

"Not to worry, Walter, I will handle this with kid gloves. I only want Henry back in one piece, and the person that is responsible in a body bag," Shaun said.

"That is exactly what I'm talking about. Let the FBI take care of bringing that one to justice, Shaun," Grooms pleaded.

"Of course I will," Shaun told him before ending the call.

Shaun drove across the airport to an older hanger that was being used by a float plane charter company, Eagle Air. He parked the rental car outside, and then went inside to see what type of plane they might be renting.

"Can I help you, sir?" A slim lady in her forties was walking across the hanger bay towards him.

"I'd like to rent a float plane for my crew and myself. We have our own pilot so all we need is the plane," Shaun told her.

"I don't let my planes out to just anyone, Mister...?" She said as she extended her hand in greeting.

"O'Brien, Shaun O'Brien," Shaun told her as he shook her hand, "My people are qualified, Miss...?"

"Just call me Dixie, Shaun, and I would need a huge deposit before we could do that kind of business. Have you got that kind of money?" Dixie asked while sizing the big man up.

"My collateral will be taxiing in here in about ten minutes, Dixie. My pilot is Navy trained and certified in both helicopter and fixed wing aircraft from F16's to Hueys," Shaun said to her.

"Well, Shaun, I've got an old DeHavilland Beaver that we might deal on," Dixie told him, "Mind you, she is not much to look at, but mechanically the old bird is perfect."

"Who does your maintenance, Dixie?" Shaun asked. He was feeling like they were on a used car lot, and Dixie was the salesman.

"Why, I do, Shaun. I own this place lock, stock, and barrel since my no good husband ran off about ten years ago. Good help is hard to find up here, so a woman has to learn to do it all or fold," she told him.

Shaun looked at her again a bit more closely. Under the dirty hands and the grease-stained coveralls was a woman of slight build, but attractive in an outdoors way. Her eyes were brown and big, and the light brown hair under her ball cap threatened to fall down at any minute. Shaun thought of how the conversation might have gone if he had been a few years younger.

"Well, don't you want to know how much?" Dixie was saying.

"I'm sorry Dixie, my mind wanders from time to time. I guess it's a sign of old age creeping up," Shaun laughed although he was slightly embarrassed.

"You don't look that old to me, Mr. O'Brien," she replied while blowing at a lock of hair that had managed to escape the hat, "Now where is your plane?"

Shaun made a call to Tuck, "Hey boy, what's your twenty?"

"We are about five minutes out just now, Shaun. Where are we going to meet?"

"Have Amos taxi over to the Eagle Air hanger when you get cleared. We have a strong lead that needs to be followed immediately," Shaun told him.

"Ten-four, we'll see you in a few," Tuck ended the call.

"They should be along any minute, Dixie. I don't know how long it will take them to clear customs, but I suspect that they are traveling light," Shaun told her.

She was looking off at the end of the main runway with her eyes shielded from the sun, "Is that your Beechcraft King Air coming in?"

"Yes, that would be my crew. Will that do as collateral on the DeHavilland?" Shaun asked.

"Shaun, that plane has always been my dream. You could have my whole fleet of two planes and a night on the town with me for that bird!" Dixie laughed.

"A few years ago, perhaps, but a woman like you needs a younger man, Dixie," Shaun blushed a little as he said it.

"Nonsense!" she exclaimed as she took his arm and led him inside the hanger, "Let's get the paperwork out of the way, and then we'll talk."

Shaun suddenly had the urge to run, but he allowed her to drag him into the office area which consisted of a counter that was built in the front of a side door. He knew now how a big fish felt as it was drawn up to the boat with a thin line.

"How do you want to pay for the rental, Shaun?" She asked as she slid the paperwork across the counter.

"Cash, Dixie, and a bonus if there is no paperwork," Shaun replied.

She just stood there and looked him over closely, this time noticing the scarred hands, the nose that had been broken several times, and the scars that had at first looked like age lines on his weathered face. She also noticed a sadness in the cold blue eyes that looked back at her as if to say "another time and place, perhaps."

"Am I going to have to patch up any bullet holes, Shaun?" she tried to joke.

"We have our own doctor on standby, and one of us usually does the patching...oh...you meant to the plane," Shaun replied, "I'll be straight up with you Dixie. A very good friend of ours is missing, and we have reason to believe that he might be alive and somewhere up near Bull Harbor. That's all that I can tell you, but I want to reassure you that you'll get the plane back in good shape, plus some cash in your pocket."

He was relieved to hear Amos taxi the big Beechcraft up to the hanger and kill the engines. They walked out to meet the crew, and

Dixie got her first look at one of the best clandestine operations teams in the world.

"Amos, Tuck, Jerry, Mike, and Raleigh, meet Dixie. She is going to let us use one of her planes to fly up to Bull Harbor," Shaun told them.

They spent a few minutes shaking hands and making small talk before Shaun broke up the party.

"Dixie, we need to get a move on. How much for the plane?" he asked.

"Have you got the papers on the Beechcraft?" she replied.

"Amos, is the paperwork on the plane inside?" He asked.

"Sure is, Dad," Amos told him.

"I'm going to kill him after this trip, I swear," Shaun said to the laughter of the men.

"Well, I think about a thousand dollars and the papers for collateral," Daisy told him.

"I can't do that, Dixie," Shaun started.

"Well, why not? Is the price too high?" she asked.

"Hardly, it is not enough money to cover the wear and tear on the old girl. How about five thousand for the plane, and a twenty-five-hundred dollar bonus like we discussed?" Shaun told her as he picked up the duffle bag that Tuck had set at his feet.

"Wow, Shaun. You'd really pay that much?" Dixie stammered.

Shaun replied by handing her seventy-five hundred dollars, and the papers that Amos had retrieved from the Beechcraft.

"Well, the keys are in the plane, and she is just down on the water over there. Throw your bags in my truck and somebody can follow us down in the car.

"Us?" Tuck asked with a grin.

"Shaun and I," was the only reply that she gave as she dragged O'Brien off by the arm.

"My oh my, I never thought that I would see this day. Mr. O'Brien has got himself roped and tied or my name isn't Hurricane!" Raleigh said to no one in particular, but everyone shook their heads in agreement and stunned disbelief.

They loaded the bags in the back of Dixie's old Chevy pickup, along with the provisions that Shaun had in the trunk, courtesy of Walter Grooms. When they got to the plane, Amos busied himself with a flight pre-check while Tuck got the gear and everybody loaded. Dixie took Shaun by the arm again and stood with him until the cough of the engine signaled that they were ready to leave.

"Shaun, I know we just met, but something is happening to me that I never thought would be possible. If you feel anything at all or nothing, now would be a good time to tell me," She told him.

"Dixie, I've not felt this uncomfortable around a woman in years. When we get finished with this, let's have a quiet dinner and get to know each other a little better. How's that?" he told her.

"That's what a girl likes to hear, Mr. O'Brien," she squeezed his arm and walked to her truck without looking back.

Shaun climbed into the cockpit with Amos and buckled up, "Well, Son, let's get the hell out of here!"

"Sure thing, Dad," Amos replied with a grin from ear to ear.

"Oh shut up!" Shaun told him without looking over.

CHAPTER TWELVE

As much as Henry wanted to build a fire and warm his joints up, he knew that whoever was after him would now be looking in the vast forest that occupied the northern stretch of the large island. His best bet would be to get back to the harbor and find some local authority that he could turn himself in to. The problem was the amount of money that was being paid out to have him hunted, although the fifty large in the duffel bag might buy him a cell phone and a boat of sorts. He decided to move back toward the dock, and the strip of woods between the road and the harbor. Doing so without being spotted was a much harder task for an old fat man to undertake, especially one with a big, wolf-looking dog tagging along.

Henry loaded the magazine of the Remington and chambered a round. Even with the open sights, he was certain of being able to hit his mark at two to three hundred yards, and trouble would probably present itself much closer than that. His next task was to hide his tarp and bit of salvaged plastic from the cabin in a small stand of spruce, leaving the duffel bag full of money and the rifle to carry. The Glock was stuck in the waistband of his trousers, and the Beretta in his coat pocket with the extra rifle rounds and the spare magazine for the Glock.

He and the dog made it quietly to the road without seeing or hearing anyone, and then came the dash across the hundred feet of clear roadway top the other side. Just as he entered the woods off of the road's edge, he heard a vehicle coming at high speed down the road from the direction of the settlement. Henry ducked as low as he could, hoping to hide in the underbrush just as a truck roared past toward the dock. On its side was the logo, 'BAR HARBOR POLICE'.

"Well, Dog, I'll bet they found my friends on that boat, or they are working with the other guys. Let's move closer to the water and see if we can find anything to help get me out of here," Henry spoke softly to the dog that just looked at him with his head cocked slightly to the side.

From the cover closer to the shoreline of the harbor, Henry could make out the flashing lights of what looked to be a patrol boat that was tied up on the dock just forward of the fishing vessel, and several men that had gathered on the dock to observe whatever was going on. Henry decided to move closer, utilizing the strip of woods and brush for cover. Somehow he needed to get close to one of the law enforcement people and get their help.

With the dog staying at his heels, Henry made the two-hundred-yard stalk through the brush in thirty minutes, stopping every twenty feet or so to look and listen for any sign of pursuit. When he was still one hundred yards from the dock, he ran out of cover and sank down to study the situation up ahead. From what he could see, the crowd consisted of some native tribesmen, several Coast Guard personnel and two police officers that also appeared to be native. As he watched, a group of men carrying two body bags left the ship and loaded them on gurneys that they then pushed up the dock to a waiting ambulance.

Henry knew that the man he had seen talking to the native that morning would be close and probably watching everything unfolding also, but he couldn't see anyone in the crowd that stood out as a non-native, except perhaps the Coast Guard personnel that seemed to be running the operation. Whoever was in charge of his abduction couldn't be very pleased that their cover had been blown by the discovery of the bodies, but it was also a pretty good bet that they would step up their efforts to find him as soon as the activity on the dock died down. He decided to move away from the dock and try to cover the distance to the village before nightfall. If all went well, he would buy a cell phone from someone and get a message to Shaun, or he and the dog would head for the deep woods to the north until the next day. However it played out, Henry was determined to have a fire tonight, either in a safe home or in the forest away from his enemies.

Decisions made under the duress caused by a lack of creature comfort, while perhaps seeming to be the best possible option at the time, can sometimes bring about unintended consequences. In Henry's case, by moving off toward the settlement in hopes of finding warmth and a phone, he missed the arrival of Shaun and his crew as they landed the DeHavilland on the other side of the ship and taxied to the dock.

Shaun got out of the plane and tethered it to a cleat on the small floating dock at the end of the main pier before turning his attention to the men that were now directing their full attention on him and the men that followed him off of the plane. He waved to the policeman that seemed to be in charge, signaling his desire to talk, and then headed up the dock to meet him. Tuck and the men stayed with the plane just in case they would need to beat a hasty retreat or fight their way out of trouble.

"Excuse me, officer," Shaun started as he approached the tribal policeman, "We are looking into the disappearance of a friend of ours and heard about the unfortunate demise of the two men that were found on that ship. Would it be possible to check the identity of the bodies to see if he is one of them?"

The policeman looked at Shaun for a moment before turning his attention to the men on the dock. What was pretty obvious was that these were not businessmen out on a fishing trip, but professional fighters on a mission of sorts.

"I'm sorry, sir, but you would have to clear that with that Coast Guard Lieutenant up there, and probably with the Mounties when they show up. What did you say your name was again?" he asked.

"Shaun O'Brien, officer. Here is my card," Shaun handed him the business card for Trade Winds Antiques which was the cover for a multitude of enterprises that Henry had his fingers in.

The Indian nodded and walked up the slight grade to where the Coast Guard lieutenant was standing and handed him Shaun's card while telling him about the man's request. The two men talked back and forth for a good five minutes before the lieutenant waved for Shaun to join him, and the tribal policeman walked off in a huff to his truck.

"Hello, Lieutenant," Shaun extended his hand to the man in greeting, "I explained to the policeman that a friend of ours was missing, and we thought he might be one of the men that you found on this ship."

"Well, Mister O'Brien, it is pretty irregular for somebody to just show up with a planeload of men and want to identify a corpse that we just found a couple of hours ago. How did you know about this?" the lieutenant asked.

"There is quite a manhunt going on down in the Washington for this friend, and I was tipped off by the FBI while those men down there and I were organizing our own efforts on this side of the border," Shaun used the direct approach method.

"I see, well, I will have to call this in and get some verification. Why don't you bring your men out of the cold, and we'll form up over there in the fishery building until the Mounties arrive," he replied.

Shaun signaled to Tuck, and they all walked to the building across from the dock to wait for a verdict which wasn't long in coming. As soon as Shaun entered, the young lieutenant looked up from his cell phone conversation and stared at the men now coming through the door as if he was a kid at a parade. He was still staring as if awestruck as he handed Shaun the phone.

"The constable wants to speak to you, Sir," he said quietly and handed him the phone.

"O'Brien here," Shaun answered.

"Shaun O'Brien! This is Constable Quincy Stuart. We met on a small job in Quebec about ten years ago," he told him.

"Quincy, yes, I do remember you. Did you marry that young lady that we rescued? I seem to remember that she was certainly fond of you," Shaun said with a laugh.

"Well, I can't go into detail because my men are standing close by, but we have two children, one of whom is named Shaun!" Quincy replied, "Now listen, I am due in there in the morning to check on this obvious murder that these coast guard boys have uncovered, but I can hold off because of weather or some such. How much time do you need?"

"I think that we can cover this place in two days, Quincy. There may be some rough stuff if we run across whoever is behind this, but we'll try and keep that to a minimum," Shaun responded.

"Good, good, I'll fly in tomorrow night and wrap up our end of it. Maybe we can tip a mug for old time's sake, what do you say?" Quincy asked.

"Sounds like we have a plan. Can you cover for us here with the reservation police? I get the feeling that he wasn't too happy to have us on his turf," Shaun asked, "Oh, and Quincy, bring me a picture of little Shaun for my wallet. It would be an honor to carry that around with me,"

"Absolutely! I'll see you tomorrow," Quincy ended the call.

"Here's your phone," Shaun tossed it to the lieutenant, "Now we need to see those bodies."

"Yes, Sir," came the crisp response, "They're in the walk-in freezer in the back."

"Little Shaun?" Tuck looked around at the men who were just staring at Shaun like he had two heads.

"What? So I helped the guy meet his wife and saved his life. No big deal," he said, slightly refaced.

Hurricane summed it up with a simple, "Uh huh."

Shaun led the way to the freezer, and they dragged the two body bags out and laid them on a processing table. Fortunately, they had not frozen solid yet and were not difficult to maneuver or finish undressing.

"What are we looking for, Boss?" Jerry asked as he flipped Yuri over on his back.

"Anything that might explain how these men were killed. I'm almost certain that Henry was involved, but we need to know if he was responsible. Tuck, while we check these out, how about taking Mike and Hurricane back to the ship and see if any of the crew noticed anything. It doesn't make sense that the hold these men were in was empty," Shaun said.

"We're on it. Have you got your ears in?" he answered.

"Good idea. To tell the truth, I had forgotten that we brought our gear with us. How about finding us a ride when you get through out there?" Shaun replied and put his communication package in his ear.

Tuck gave him a 'thumbs up' and the three men left the building.

"Boss, look at this guy's neck," Jerry moved Otto's head around to show the bruise that was just below the ear in his neck. In the center of the purplish bruise was a small red dot.

Shaun took a close look at it, and the hand prints on the other side of the dead man's neck.

"Somebody injected something in here," he told Mike, "Let's look at the other stiff."

They checked the same area on Yuri and found nothing. Shaun got a towel from a rack near the cleaning sink and started wiping the oily mess off of Yuri's chest.

"Hello! Look at this, Jerry. We've got a needle mark next to his right nipple. Judging by the size of the spot, this was a Digitalis injection, although normally it would have been given through the nipple center so that it would remain untraceable," Shaun explained, "It might just be wishful thinking, but suppose that Henry managed to get his hands on that needle and drive it into this guy. He wouldn't be very concerned about hiding it, just getting it in there. I think we can say that this was not a hit on these men, but an escape attempt."

"If that is the case, where is Henry now?" Jerry asked.

"Somewhere close, I imagine," Shaun replied, "Let's get these guys back in the bags and in the freezer, then we'll go find the rest of the crew and come up with a search plan."

Henry decided to cut across the road and head north, into the densest part of the island in hopes of finding a bit of safety in the forest. He was in need of a fire and some shelter of sorts. Water was also a problem, and it wouldn't be long before his body shut down over the lack of it. Once he and the dog, who apparently had adopted him, were safely out of sight of prying eyes, he would try to set up a base camp to forage from with his first mission focused on finding water.

About a quarter of a mile into the wood, Henry cut across a vehicle track that appeared to be fairly fresh so he followed it carefully, stopping every few feet to survey the area ahead of him. Several hundred yards later, he saw an old cabin buried in the undergrowth, but with smoke coming from the stove pipe stack in the roof. He also saw the hackles on the Malamute stand up as the dog took in the scene ahead of them.

"I get the same feeling, fella. Let's wait out here for a bit and see if anyone leaves," he spoke softly to the animal and moved off into some heavy cover.

The tactic paid off about an hour later when the rattling of the vehicle that made the tracks could be heard coming through the woods. Henry put his hand on the dog's neck to keep him from bolting, and they lay still in the cover as the old truck rattled past. As soon as it pulled up to the cabin, two men with rifles ran out to meet it. After a few minutes of talking through the window, they both got into the cab and left with the driver. Henry noticed that neither of these men looked like natives, but he couldn't see the driver well enough to tell.

As soon as they left, he moved slowly to the back of the cabin and looked in one of the dirty windows next to the back door. There wasn't any sound or movement, so after about five minutes, Henry decided to enter the place and have a look. Entering at the unlocked backdoor brought him into the kitchen area where there was a large plastic jug of water sitting on a shaky wooden structure that passed as a table. Henry picked up a dirty coffee cup and helped himself to a drink before finding a pan to put some in for the dog. Mindful that these people might be back at any moment, he then eased through the other large room that was stacked with boxes and some clothes that had been thrown across an old couch.

Henry opened one of the boxes and found some of the medical equipment that had been on the ship. He stood still for a minute letting the knowledge that he now had an upper hand on his captors sink in to his thoughts. Up until now, his instinct was one for flight and survival, but now his thoughts turned to retribution. Henry quickly looked through the boxes, being careful to close them as he had found them, and then turned his attention to the clothes on the sofa. A very expensive cashmere car coat that was buried under some hang-up clothes caught his attention. He pulled it out and looked at the label which read, 'Tailored for Walter Grooms by Winston Clothiers of Seattle'.

Henry stood still for a minute letting this new found information soak in. He knew that Walter Grooms was an FBI Special Agent in Seattle because Henry had been instrumental in getting that position for him after Grooms had helped fake the deaths of Tuck and his family three years before.

The obvious question to Henry was, "What was Grooms doing here?", and he thought that he knew the answer, but for now, he had to get clear of the cabin and into a shelter so he could think. Henry went back into the kitchen and found two plastic gallon jugs that he filled with water from the large one on the table. It wouldn't do to tip his hand by taking all of their water, and two gallons would last him and the dog for no longer than he intended to be here. He also found some more dried salmon and a few cans of beanie weenies that he put into his pockets. Once that was done, he left the cabin and continued north further into the forest, and away from danger.

CHAPTER THIRTEEN

Hanna woke up from her long afternoon nap and found Maggie sitting in the huge living room with Abigail, Bob, and the children.

"Hi everybody," she said as she walked into the room, "I'm sorry to have flaked out like that, and I do appreciate you guys taking care of the children. I'd better feed Michael though, he's overdue."

"I gave him some of the frozen milk about a half hour ago, Hanna. Why don't you sit and talk to us while Emily and Bob round us up something to eat?" Abigail asked her.

"Momma, 'Uncle' Bob and I can fix lunch, can't we Uncle Bob?" Emily blurted out.

"Yes, we can, Emily. What do you want?" Bob took his cue from Abigail.

"Grilled cheese, grilled cheese," Emily ran to the kitchen.

"How about grilled cheese and tomato soup...if there is any in there?" Bob asked with a laugh.

"Anything will be great, Bob. I didn't know how hungry I was," Hanna answered, suddenly looking more like the old Hanna.

"With the great helper that I've got, it will be coming right up!" he laughed and followed the sound of a little voice yelling for 'Uncle' Bob.

"Maggie, have you heard from Amos since they left?" Hanna asked.

"Just about an hour ago they flew into some remote place close to Vancouver Island, but he couldn't tell me where. You know how those men are. Everything is top secret," Maggie laughed,

"He did tell me that Shaun thought that Henry was close by, and that they should know something before morning."

"Thank God for that!" Abigail exclaimed, "It will be nice to get out of here and do a little 'expensive' shopping before we go back to the church."

"Shopping? Now that would be a novelty. Tuck has promised me a trip to New York City after all of this is over. Why don't we all go?" she asked around.

Abigail and Maggie laughed, but they both agreed that they were in on the trip.

"Hey what are you all laughing at?" Bob stuck his head back in the room, "I've got chicken noodle and some killer extra sharp Cuba, New York cheese. How many sandwiches can you girls eat?"

"Nothing, Bob. We are just conspiring against your wallet," Abigail told him, "Fix us a couple each, Dear, and make sure to cut the crust off Emily's. I seem to remember them that way when I was little."

"Hanna, if we can get back to a more or less normal life, what is the first thing you want to do after the shopping trip?" Maggie asked.

"Hmmm..., I want to go back to Myrtle Beach and see Kathryn, and my sisters too, of course. Then I want Tuck to buy us a little house with some acreage maybe somewhere just north of the beach. Emily and I could have such a good time there while Tuck runs the woods with Michael Junior," she responded.

"I think that I've had enough of the big time for a good while. I'd like to write something and have more time to spend with Amos when Shaun isn't having him fly off to Timbuktu all of the time. Being around you and the children is doing something to my maternal instincts, so who knows?" Maggie laughed, "What about you, Abigail? What do you guys want to do?"

"Girls, Bob and I are very happy working in the mission back home, and while I am glad to take a little break, we really want to be just where the Lord wants us to be. Neither of us are spring chickens either, so a little excitement goes a long way with me," Abigail let her mind drift back to the Tennessee cabin where she had been held captive not so long ago.

Their reverie was interrupted by, "COME AND GET IT," emanating from the kitchen.

The rest of the next hour was spent with Hanna taking turns between eating and helping Emily, plus feeding baby Michael. Maggie stepped in like a new mother herself and took Emily in to give her a bath after they had eaten. Bob and Abigail found themselves alone at the table.

"Well, Kid, I cooked, are you going to clean?" he teased.

"I've never met a man as messy as you are in the kitchen, Bob," Abigail pretended to scold him.

"Well, you know what the bible says," he laughed.

"Yes, I do, but you are going to tell me anyway, aren't you?" She had heard it a thousand times before.

"Where there are no oxen the stable is clean, but much increase comes by the strength of the ox. In this case, soup and sandwiches," he laughed.

"You know that I only put up with you because you can cook...right?" she laughed back at him.

"Hanna doesn't seem as withdrawn, does she?" Bob asked.

"I think that time will tell, Bob. She has been through a lot of pain and is still coping with it. If everything returns to normal, whatever that was after Tuck gets back, I think she'll be well on her way to healing," Abigail responded.

"Then we need to double up on the prayers for all of this to be over," Bob said as he squeezed her hand.

The buzzer on the intercom interrupted them, and a voice called out, "Mister Pike...Mister Pike, can you hear me?"

Bob jumped up and quickly made his way to the device, "Bob Pike here, what's going on?"

"Mr. Pike, Tuck told us that you could handle a weapon. We've got some suspicious activity outside, and might need a little help," the voice said, "Please get the women into the safe room and use the stairwell. We are securing the elevator."

"I'll be right down," Bob replied, and then to Abigail, "Better start that praying now!"

Abigail ran to where the others were with the children and told them what was going on.

"We need to get in the safe room, now!" she told them, "Bob is going down to help the men if anything happens."

"I'll be going down too," Hanna told her, "If you can take care of my babies until I get back, I'd appreciate it."

"Of course, Hanna, but do you think that is wise?" Maggie asked.

"Wise or not, I'm not going to sit up here and just hope that everything turns out all right," she replied, "Wait up Bob, I'm coming with you."

She hugged the children and then ran to the room where Tuck had put their bags to retrieve his drag bag with the .308 custom

Remington that he almost never left behind. Slinging the rifle over her shoulder, the slender woman walked briskly to the door that Bob Pike was holding for them.

"We'll be back in a few minutes, I'm certain," Bob called out even though he wasn't.

Hanna was busy loading the magazine of the 700 Remington as they walked down the stairs, and had the bolt ready to close on a loaded chamber when they reached the bottom.

Tony, one of the two men that Tuck had left in charge stared at Hanna with a look of shock on his face.

"Excuse me, Hanna, but I don't think that Tuck would want you down here," He told her.

"Tuck isn't here now is he, Tony?" she answered defiantly, "Now tell me where you want me to be."

"Over on the catwalk where you can cover the street without being seen. There is a convoy of black cars coming by about every five minutes," he pointed to the area, "Mr. Pike, what type of weapon do you prefer?"

"Call me Bob, Tony. I can handle anything that you've got, but I prefer prayer," Bob tried to joke.

"Well say a couple for George and me when you do," he laughed, "I'll get you an M-4 and some rounds."

True to their observations, three black SUVs pulled up on the opposite side of the street, and a man fashionably dressed stepped out to survey the top floors of the block-long building with a set of binoculars. He spent five full minutes looking before handing them back to someone unseen inside of the car and then walked across the street to the building front and the rusted steel door that looked like it hadn't been opened in many years.

"This guy has some big ones, eh Bob?" Tony whispered.

"I think he has a message for us, Tony. Look how he is holding his coat open to show that he is unarmed," Bob replied, "At least where we can see, anyway."

"Let's see what he does," Tony replied.

Hanna had a round in the chamber and the crosshairs of the .308 on the driver of the lead SUV, but her safety was still on and her finger wasn't on the trigger, Bob noted with relief. She was a loose cannon as far as he was concerned, and anything might set her off.

"HELLO IN THE BUILDING," The stranger suddenly shouted, "I HAVE A MESSAGE FOR MR. O'BRIEN. YOU HAVE TWENTY-FOUR HOURS TO DELIVER HANNA TUCKER TO US, OR WE WILL BURN THIS ENTIRE BLOCK!"

Tony and George looked at Hanna for a second before Tony asked, "Who did you piss off, Hanna?"

Hanna was still calm like a bomb right before it explodes, "Probably something to do with those cartel men that I killed in Texas, and the deranged sister up in Idaho."

She now had the crosshairs trained on the back of the man's head as he walked back across the street. Bob saw her ease the safety off and watched as her finger moved inside of the trigger guard.

"Don't kill him, Hanna!" he exclaimed, "We still have twenty-four hours and a slight advantage if we don't show our hand."

Hanna didn't respond, but the man got to the car and turned to give a last look before entering. Only then did she lift her head from the rifle stock and put the safety back on.

Bob breathed a sigh of relief before asking Tony, "Have you got Shaun's emergency number? We need to let him know what's going on."

"Yes, Sir," he replied and dug out the phone.

"Shaun answered on the first ring, "Hello, Tony, what's up?"

"Not Tony, Shaun, this is Bob Pike. We had a visit from someone a few minutes ago, and he delivered an ultimatum to you. He wants Hanna in twenty-four hours, or he burns the block," Bob told him.

"Well, on the upside, we can probably deduce that it is cartel related since Hanna took out most of their leadership. The situation is not as bleak as it might look. There is a tunnel system under the building that runs for two blocks to another building that we use for a business cover. Get everybody ready to move on short notice, and hand the phone back to Tony," Shaun told him.

Bob gave Tony the phone back and signaled to Hanna to come down from the catwalk, "It's under control, Hanna. Let's go back upstairs."

"What did Shaun say?" she asked as he helped her down.

"He said that we are not to worry, that here is an escape tunnel system under the building that will get us out of here if need be. Tony is going to handle that, and I think we need to get back upstairs where the girls are probably worried sick," he replied.

George signaled for them to take the elevator, and a very grim looking Hanna got on, followed by a very worried looking Bob Pike.

Shaun and Jerry had just finished loading the bodies back in the makeshift morgue when the phone call came in about the intrusion at the safe house.

"Jerry, we've been found out back in Miami. There was a crew at the house demanding that Hanna be turned over to them. This whole thing has to be retribution for Hanna killing that Salinas woman three years ago," Shaun told him.

"Do we need to load up and get back there, Shaun?" Jerry asked.

"We need to find Henry first. They gave a twenty-four-hour window for her surrender, and we need to make the most of that time up here," he responded, "Let's go find Tuck."

CHAPTER FOURTEEN

Henry Albright stopped to rest about three hundred yards from the shack where he had found Walter Grooms' coat. The two water jugs had been tied together at the neck with a piece of liberated rope, and it had begun to dig into his shoulders.

"Take a break, Fella," he said to the dog that followed his every move.

He sat on a large fallen tree trunk and broke a piece of salmon off for both him and the dog before opening one of the cans of Beanie Weenies.

"When we get out of here, I'm buying you the biggest steak that I can find," he said to the dog who just cocked his head to the side as he looked at him.

Henry glanced around the place where they had stopped and saw what looked like a drop in the forest floor a few yards to the north. He slowly dragged himself up and walked over to take a look. Running East and West from where he was standing was a rift in the floor of the forest that must have been caused by an ages old earthquake which had thrown one side of a fault, the side Henry was on, up about fifteen feet higher than the other side. To his right, a massive spruce had fallen several years before and now lay parallel to the rift, close to the bottom, making a natural shelter from both the weather and from prying eyes.

"Let's go down there and check this out," Henry said to his companion as he hurriedly gathered his things and half climbed, half slid down to the fallen tree.

He cleaned dead limbs and debris that had accumulated under the tree before ending up with a fairly comfortable cave big enough for the two of them to crawl into. His next act was to build a fire pit and make a small fire close to the mouth of the hide so he could finally get warm. There was enough fallen limbs and other wood close at hand to fuel a small fire through the night, and he didn't intend to set up housekeeping for much longer than it took to find a phone and a way off of the island. Henry stashed the case with the money in one end of the cave, taking care to cover it with dead leaves, after removing several hundred dollars for 'necessary' expenses. The crackling fire gradually knocked the cold chill off, and Henry was starting to feel like a new man. That is he would have except for the clothes that he had taken from Yuri stank when he got them, and now they could practically stand on their own. Henry stuck the Glock in his coat pocket and picked up the 30-06.

"Let's go find us a phone, Dog," he said quietly, "If you are going to hang out with me, you need a name. How about Harry? My late brother would get a kick out of it!"

The upright bushy tail, characteristic of the Malamute, wagged back and forth.

"Harry it is! Come on then, let's go find these people that want to do me in. I'll wager that before the end of the day, they will regret that they jumped on that job offer," Henry got another drink for both of them, kicked dirt over the fire, and then started off back in the direction of the town.

The sound of the truck returning to the cabin alerted them to possible danger, so Henry changed his direction and headed towards the sound. He might as well do what he could to even the odds a bit instead of having to take on a crowd by himself.

Besides, one of these buggers might have some cleaner underwear than what he had on at the present.

He made the distance back to the shack unnoticed just as the truck with two men onboard was pulling up, so they crouched behind a large tree and waited for them to get out of the old pickup.

"Keep down, Harry," he whispered to the dog.

Henry listened closely for the conversation to reveal what he might be up against, but all that he heard was one of them say to the other, "It's your fault that the money disappeared, not mine!" just as they made it through the front door.

Well, at least he knew that these had something to do with his predicament. It was time to unleash a little hell on them. Henry looked around carefully for any sign of others in the woods before creeping up to the cabin door. He could hear them arguing about something through the door just before he pushed it open with a crash.

The tall greasy looking man closest to Henry spun around in surprise and terror with a knife in his hand while the other reached for a pistol in a waistband holster. The butt of the old Remington smashed into the face of the knife wielder, dropping him instantly like he was a pole-axed steer. Henry let go of the rifle with his right hand and drew the Glock up, firing from a half raised position just as the other brought his weapon to bear. The 10mm round from the Glock caught the unfortunate man just below the sternum and right of center, knocking him back into a pile of boxes. Henry started to finish him off with a second round before seeing the blood running from his mouth and nose in a torrent. He kicked the man's pistol out of reach and knelt beside him.

"Who are you working for?" he asked.

The man gurgled through the blood, "Piss off!"

"You will be dead in a few minutes. Tell me who you are working for!" Henry pressed him for an answer.

The man just gave him a bloody grin as his head bowed down on his chest.

Henry turned his attention to the first man that was groaning behind him. He picked up the man's knife from where it lay on the floor and grabbing him by the collar, dragged him out of the door of the shack and into the light.

Henry propped the dazed man up in a seated position against the wood pile on the cabin porch before asking him the same question that he had asked the other, "Who are you working for?"

The man just looked at Henry and smiled but said nothing.

Slowly, Henry shoved the five-inch bladed knife to the hilt in the joint of the man's right shoulder, giving it a little twist before pulling it out just as slowly. The man's eyes rolled back in his head as he screamed in pain, and he threw his left hand over the wound, which was bleeding profusely.

"Now...let's start all over again, friend. Who...are...you...working...for?" Henry dragged the question out slowly.

"Please, I'm going to bleed out." he responded.

"Most definitely, but not for at least twenty minutes or so if you keep your hand over it. Now answer my question before you spring another leak!" Henry's voice was cold as ice.

"Grooms, a man named Grooms hired us to take you off the ship and deliver you to him. That's all I know...honest!" he sobbed.

"How many of you are there?" Henry asked another question.

"Five, there's five of us. We were to get ten grand a piece when you were delivered. I swear that's all I know. Please get me some help," The man begged.

"One more question and then you can go find help. Where is Walter Grooms now?" Henry asked.

"I don't know. In the village somewhere, but I haven't seen him since this morning. He is planning a trap for the men that flew in this morning and started asking questions about the two men they found in the ship," he answered weakly.

"When did you say these men arrived?" Henry was startled.

"This morning just after the Coast Guard took the bodies off of the ship," the man was growing weaker.

Henry smiled a big smile. The cavalry had arrived. It had to be Shaun in that plane, and Henry needed to get to him without getting killed first.

"Thanks for the info. You've been a real sport," he told the man who was slowly bleeding to death, "Now where is your cell phone?"

"I don't have one. Aren't you going to get me to a doctor?" the man asked.

"I'm not going to kill you, so you had better start walking," Henry told him.

Henry ducked back inside of the shack and rummaged the dead one's pockets until he found the truck keys, but no phone, stopping briefly to grab Groom's coat before walking out past the man on the porch.

"Come on, Harry," he said to the dog as headed for the truck. Harry cocked his head at Henry's command, then raised his leg to relieve himself on the whimpering man.

"I wanted to do that myself," Henry said when the dog climbed into the truck with him, "Let's go get my bag and then find Shaun!"

CHAPTER FIFTEEN

Maggie took one look at the scowl on Hanna's face when they came through the door and knew that something was dreadfully wrong.

"Hanna, what is it?" She asked.

"I'm just fed up with this whole thing, and there is no way to get out of it that I can see!" Hanna shouted to no one in particular.

Her shouting woke baby Michael and started Emily crying softly.

"We need to keep calm and get our stuff together. Shaun wants us to leave by way of a tunnel system under the building. To where exactly, I'm not sure," Bob told them.

Abigail picked up little Michael, and Maggie shushed Emily with a hug while Hanna stormed off to their bedroom.

"What's happening, Bob?" Maggie asked in a hushed tone.

"It looks like it is some cartel that is after Hanna for killing a couple of their family members in Texas," Bob answered.

"For Pete's sake, they were trying to kill her and a friend of theirs on the ranch out there. Hanna saved his life," she replied.

"Well, they know we're here now, and we've got to put a little distance between us and this building before tomorrow when they come back to burn it!" Bob exclaimed.

"I'll get our bag packed, Bob," Abigail came back from the kitchen with a bottle in Junior's mouth, "Ministry is so much more relaxing than being a game warden, isn't it?"

"Well, on the bright side, it gives you more opportunities for prayer, and that is a good thing," Bob laughed.

Hanna came back in the room, "I'm sorry about screaming at everyone. Something seems to be wrong with me, kind of like I'm out of control sometimes."

Abigail handed the baby over, "Hanna, you have been through more than most combat veterans have, and your emotions are frayed a bit. That's all. We'll get through this together and have some really tall tales tell your grandchildren."

"I hope that you're right Abigail. Right now I don't think that I've ever felt further from the Lord or more empty," Hanna said quietly and walked back to the bedroom with the baby.

"I think we'll go ahead and leave, so try to get everybody ready while I check with the men on the details," Bob told them and walked back out.

"Abigail, I'm worried about Hanna," Maggie said quietly when Bob left.

"She'll be fine, Maggie, just as soon as we can get this behind us, and the dust clears. How about you? Are you okay?" she asked.

"I'm not having emotional instability if that's what you mean, but I do feel unsettled inside most of the time, even when Amos is around. Is that strange?" Maggie replied.

"Not at all. When you get to where that doesn't bother you, then you will be too far gone spiritually for God to help," Abigail counseled.

"I haven't thought much about God since, well for a long time," Maggie admitted, "Is it too late for me to start now? I hate to just use Him when I'm in trouble," she responded.

"We've got a few minutes, Maggie, and I think God wants to hear from you now. Would you mind if I prayed with you?"

Abigail sat down on the sofa and took Emily out of Maggie's arms where the child had fallen asleep.

"I would like that very much," Maggie said with tears in her eyes and her voice breaking.

Bob Pike reached the ground floor and found Tony with George and six other men.

"Hello Bob, are you folks ready to make the run?" Tony asked when he looked up and saw him standing there.

"I suppose so, but what is the plan, exactly, and where did all of these men come from?" Bob asked.

"We are planning a surprise party for our guests out there when they come back. Shaun wouldn't take kindly to us letting his house burn down, would he?" George laughed, "You folks are going through the tunnel which ends at a set of elevator doors. That will take you to a parking garage where a van is waiting with the keys under the floor mat. I've reprogrammed the GPS unit to take you to the next safe house where you will find clothes, cell phones, and food enough for several days if need be."

"I'll go get the girls and be back down in a half an hour," Bob told him, "Should I stay and help out here?"

"We appreciate it, Sir, but the boys would take it kind of hard if you cut into their action," George told him with a grin while the others broke out in laughter.

"Truthfully, I'm glad that you answered that way. I'm not as young as I once was," Bob shook his hand and returned to the upstairs.

It was now crunch time, and Bob wished that Tuck was here to help protect the families. He felt like leaving the safe house, which suddenly wasn't very safe, left them with few options. Bob reached the apartment just as Abigail finished praying with Maggie, and Hanna came out of the bedroom with her bag and the baby.

"You girls ready to go?" Bob asked.

"Ready as we ever are, I suppose," Hanna quipped sarcastically, "Let's see what adventure life is going to throw at us next!"

"That's the spirit, Hanna. How about everybody else?" he asked, ignoring the sarcasm.

"Give us about ten minutes, Bob," Abigail told him, "Maggie and I want to freshen up a bit before we get out in public again."

Bob took Emily while the women headed for the ladies' room, and Hanna joined him on the sofa with the baby.

"Bob, do you think that we'll get out of this. I mean really out of this?" Hanna asked.

"Only God knows the answer to that one, Hanna, and He hasn't seen fit to tell me, yet," Bob tried to joke to hide his concern.

"I'm just so tired of living one day at a time and never knowing when the call is going to come like the one we got the other day on the island. It's hard to just pick up and leave everything behind, and now we've done it several times since Daddy died," Hanna had tears in her eyes.

"The only advice that I can give you is what I've been following myself. Work the problem like it is up to you to solve it, and pray like it is up to God. I firmly believe that He will not let us down, no matter how dark it looks," Bob responded.

Abigail came back with Maggie following, "Okay, Bob, we are ready to leave!"

"What about the rifle?" Hanna asked Bob, "Shouldn't we take it with us?"

"I think that we will okay without it. Besides, if there are any people in that parking garage, it will throw up a real red flag," Bob told her.

The ride down the elevator to the first-floor garage was made in silence. Tony met them at the door and got in.

"We are going further down from here, folks. The door will open on the tunnel. From there, you just walk to the next set of doors and get in that elevator. Push the 'P' button, and you will end up in the garage of an office building. Your van sticks out like a sore thumb and will be easy to find. Best of luck," Tony told them as the door opened on a well-lit, concrete tunnel that stretched off into the distance.

"Thanks, Tony. We appreciate all that you men have done," Bob shook his hand.

"It's been a pleasure, folks. Now head on off, they'll be needing me back before the party starts," he laughed.

The doors closed, leaving the group standing in a long hallway, looking off into the distance as if each was afraid to take the first step.

"Emily, how about a pony ride to the next elevator?" Bob asked, and Emily climbed up on his back.

"That's our signal, ladies," Abigail caught up with her husband as the others walked gloomily along behind.

They walked for what seemed like an hour but was closer to fifteen minutes, before seeing the elevator door at the end of the tunnel. All there was to do now was press the button for the elevator and wait. They heard the sound of the elevator car reach a position up a level from them, and then go back up three times before it came all the way down and stopped. When the doors opened they all breathed a sigh of relief that it was empty.

"They must have programmed it not to come down here from one of the upper floors," Bob told them, "Well, let's go find our ride."

The doors opened on a plain lower level garage that would be indistinguishable from any other business in Miami. The only thing that made this one stand out was an older Ford F-350 church van that was backed into a space close to the elevator marked 'reserved'. On the sides of the dark gray van were the large block letters spelling out in screaming white, 'FIRST IN FAITH ASSEMBLY, ANDYTOWN, FLORIDA'.

"I'll bet that's us," Bob said quietly.

"I'm afraid your right, dear," Abigail responded.

"In we go then, ladies," Bob opened the unlocked side door. Abigail got into the passenger side, while Maggie and Hanna took the children to the center section.

Bob opened the driver's door and found the keys under the mat where they had been stashed. Fearing the worst, he turned the engine over, expecting a cough and a cloud of blue smoke to accompany the starting. What he was greeted by instead was the healthy roar of the big 415 cubic inch V-10 as it cranked on the first turn of the starter.

"I think this is no ordinary van, ladies. As soon as the GPS comes online, we'll get out of here," he told them.

They maneuvered through traffic to the drone of the voice on the GPS and soon found themselves on West Okeechobee Road, headed to a place called Andytown about forty-five miles away.

"What's in Andytown, I wonder?" Bob said out loud.

"I've never heard of it," Abigail answered from the back, "but, then again, I've never been here before."

Maggie spoke up, "I just looked it up on my map app, and it looks like there is nothing there except an interchange. Are we going in the right direction?"

"I suppose we'll know when we get there," Bob answered, "Why don't you look around the van and see if there is any equipment in here for survival.

Hanna and Maggie checked all of the pockets before Hanna put her hand under the back seat.

"Hello!" she exclaimed as she came out with a travel bag full of something.

"What have you got?" Bob asked, looking in the mirror.

"I don't know, but it is heavy," she replied before dumping the contents on the seat.

In the bag were two cell phones, twenty thousand dollars in twenties and tens, a set of house keys, and an Armscor 1911 .45ACP with two mags and a note attached.

"Well, what does it say?" Maggie and Abigail asked simultaneously.

"It says, 'Shaun thought that you might need this. The pistol is for Bob. Call the pre-programmed number when you reach the house.' That's all," Hanna told them.

"Well, at least there is supposed to be a house. That's something anyway," Maggie laughed nervously.

"Everybody settle down now. I have a feeling that everything is going to be all right before too very long," Bob told them.

The V-10 thundered up the highway for another thirty miles before the GPS gave them the instructions to take I-24 to the right.

Twenty minutes later, they were pulling into the driveway of a small home immediately adjacent to a two-story, white concrete block church with a sign that said 'FIRST IN FAITH ASSEMBLY'.

"We have arrived!" Bob made the announcement as he shut off the van, "Let's go knock on the door and see if anyone is home."

CHAPTER SIXTEEN

Tuck and his team searched every square inch of the fish hold where they believed that Henry must have been held but found no evidence that it had been used for anything other than a fish hold for years.

"Hurricane, why don't you use your persuasive nature on the crew members that we passed coming in here and see if their memories can't be jogged a little bit?" Tuck spoke to the big man with a little humor in his voice, "Mike and I will keep looking down here and then join you."

"How much persuasion can I use?" The question was straight forward.

"Try not to leave any marks," was Tuck's reply.

Tuck watched as Hurricane exited through the hatch, and then started to leave himself when a small piece of paper by the hatch caught his attention. To his surprise, it was a label for a bottle of sodium thiopental. Bingo! Now they knew for certain that something other than fish had passed through this hold and that something had to be Henry Albright, but where was he?

"Shaun, do you have a copy on me?" Tuck asked into his electronics.

"I can hear you, Tuck, what's going on?" came the reply into his ear.

"I've got a label for some nasty knockout drops that we missed down here. Mike is bringing it over," he responded.

"Here you go, Mike. Get this to Shaun and keep your sonar on for anything out of the ordinary," Tuck handed him the paper.

"What is ordinary about this place?" Mike asked.

"Anything not Indian related, maybe several non-natives traveling together," Tuck explained, "I'm going to give Hurricane a hand."

Whether or not the mountain of a man they called 'Hurricane' needed a hand wasn't immediately obvious from the noise that was coming from forward of the gangway that Mike took to exit the ship. Tuck jogged to where the noise was coming from another hatch and found three men trying to rough Hurricane up in what appeared to be the galley.

None of the participants saw him enter the small area, so Tuck just took a seat on the edge of a table and watched as, one by one, Hurricane laid the men out like cordwood with well-placed blows to their heads.

"Need some help, Big Guy?" Tuck laughed.

"I could have used some a few minutes ago. That greasy looking one stuck a knife in me when I came in!" he replied.

"Let me look at it," Tuck replied switching places with his teammate, "Well, it missed gutting you for sure. I think he only got the muscle on your waist. Do we need to get to the hospital, or can Shaun sew you up until we get back?"

"I'm not hurt that bad, just put some gauze in it from that first aid kit, and I'll be good to go," he answered pointing to the kit on the galley bulkhead, "That one there knows something that we need to know, Tuck. He wouldn't have attacked me like that otherwise."

Tuck turned his attention to the taller of the men on the deck at their feet and prodded him with his toe. When there was no response, Tuck reached down and got a wad of hair in his hand which he used to drag the man into an upright position.

"All right, all right, you don't have to do that. I'm cooperating," were his first words as Tuck slammed him into a seat at the table.

"Tell me who you are working for," Tuck asked menacingly.

"No way, he'll kill me," he replied.

"What do you think that I am going to do with you?" Tuck answered, "You really don't have much to choose from, but your boss will probably kill you quickly, whereas we will keep you alive by transfusions if necessary, until you tell us what we want to know."

"I just can't tell you anything, mister. My family would be in danger too," came the whining plea.

Suddenly, Hurricane plunged the knife that had cut him through the forearm of the suspect between the bones, and deep into the wooden table top. Tuck got up and closed the galley door to dampen the man's screams to the outside. Hurricane went through the various drawers and came back to the sobbing man with two large white handled butcher knives that he'd found. He grabbed the man's free hand and pulled it toward him across the table.

"Now, I believe the boss asked you a pretty simple question. If you don't want the other arm pinned to this table, I need to hear an answer!" he told him.

Tuck dragged the other two men to a lazarette at the far end of the galley and locked them in before returning to the interrogation and taking one of the knives from Hurricane. He reached the counter where a steel was hanging and worked the blade across its surface until it was razor sharp. None of this was missed by the wild-eyed man slobbering in pain at the table.

"I'll tell you what I know. Please don't hurt me anymore," he sobbed.

"Start talking, trash. We haven't got all day!" Hurricane admonished him.

"We were hired by a man in Seattle that is working for Julius Salinas of the Los Zetas cartel to transport Henry Albright from Washington to here. Sometime after we docked, Albright got loose and killed the two that they found earlier. I've got men out looking for him in town and in the woods, but nobody has seen anything. That's all I know, I swear!" he cried.

"Give me the name of the Seattle contact," Tuck told him.

"I don't know, but he got in here about thirty minutes before you guys did," was the answer, "He said it was time to spring the trap...whatever that means."

"We need to go, Hurricane. This one has told us what we need to know," Tuck said.

"What about me? You can't just leave me pinned to this table. I'll bleed to death," Cried Greasy.

"Should have thought of that before you stuck your blade in me," Hurricane answered gruffly and followed Tuck outside.

"Shaun, come in," Tuck worked the electronics.

"Go ahead Tuck," Shaun answered in his ear piece.

"I think we have some problems, Shaun. If this guy that we've questioned is to be believed, we've walked into a trap!" Tuck told him.

"Get on back here and you can tell me what you've learned. Is Henry still alive?" Shaun asked.

"I think that he must be. This guy has half the island looking for him," Tuck answered, "Is Amos back there yet? He went looking for some transportation."

"Not yet, I'll give him a buzz and see what the holdup is," came the reply in Tuck's ear.

"I'm on the way back with something that resembles a truck," Amos' voice came through the earpieces, "I've got something else too...be there in five minutes."

Tuck and Hurricane made the run back to the fish house without incident just as Amos pulled the old beater Chevrolet up in a cloud of blue smoke and a squeal of brake linings. There in the front seat with Amos and a big dog was a bedraggled Henry Albright looking like he hadn't slept in months.

"Hey nephew, I wasn't sure that your smiling face was something that I'd ever see again," Henry spoke to Tuck when he got out of the truck, "Is Shaun around? I've got something important for him."

"He's inside, Uncle Henry. Let Hurricane and I give you a hand," Tuck replied as he signaled with his head for Hurricane to take Henry's other arm.

"Obliged, Tuck, I don't have much energy left after the last few days," Henry replied.

They made the walk to the cabin with Amos watching their backs. Tuck kicked the door open.

"I've got a surprise for you, Shaun. The boss has shown up!" he shouted.

"Henry!" Shaun exclaimed as he gave the big man a hug of friendship, "You had us worried."

"I had me worried too, Shaun, but this isn't time for celebration. Walter Grooms is up here, and he means to kill you!"

"Grooms, you're certain that Grooms is behind this?" Shaun asked, "He was the one that sent us up here to find you."

"He gave you the lead so that all of you would be together, and in his trap," Henry told him, tossing Groom's coat over, "Have any of you got some clean underwear? Something is having a party in my shorts!"

"I've got something that might fit you, sir," Hurricane spoke up as he dug out a pair from his bag.

"Thank God, I was thinking that the itching would never stop!" Henry laughed, "We've not met formally, I'm Henry Albright, and you are?

"Raleigh Evans, sir. My friends call me Hurricane," he replied with an outstretched hand holding the underwear.

"Hurricane it is!" Henry laughed as he took the underwear and shook the massive hand, "I'm thinking that there must be some hot water in here. Let me go find something to wash off with and get into my boxers."

Henry went into the back room to clean up and the men discussed a plan of action now that their enemy had been identified. They were interrupted by a scratching on the door which turned out to be the Malamute looking for Henry.

"What's this, another team member?" Shaun asked.

A voice from the other room answered back, "That's my partner, 'Harry'. He's already kept me out of trouble. I'm going to buy him a steak when we get back."

Tuck scratched the soft hair behind the dog's ears for a moment before saying, "We probably should post a perimeter watch if these guys are looking for us. I don't want to be taken by surprise in this drafty shack."

"Good idea, Tuck. Take the men and get us some eyes on the road coming in. Amos, how about getting over to the plane and get her ready for departure," Shaun replied.

The men left just as Henry came out of the back of the fish house, "I took care of two of Grooms' men back in the woods. One of them told me that Grooms had five men with him. That leaves three plus him."

"Tuck and Hurricane disabled one over on the ship so I'm thinking there are two plus Grooms," Shaun replied, "Amos is getting the DeHavilland ready so we can go ahead and get out of here before they show up."

Shaun's ear bud went off, "Shaun, they've sunk the plane! One of the pontoons is punctured, and she's lying on her side."

"Well, crap! Amos, work your way up on the fishing boat and give us some cover from the upper level. Don't let anyone back on or off that ship. Tuck, did you copy that?" Shaun asked.

"Yes, sir, I'm on the way there with Jerry. You know that our heavy arms are on that plane, right?" Tuck answered.

"See what you can do down there. We'll be along shortly," Shaun finished, "Well, that kind of blows our escape plan wide open. If we can hang out until tomorrow night, Constable Quincy will be here, but I've got a feeling it will be too late to help us. I really want to get all of these men off this island!"

"Let's get everybody to that ship. At least it is a bit more bullet proof than this shack," Henry answered.

Shaun gave the necessary orders for the men to fall back to the fishing vessel, and then he and Henry accompanied by the Malamute got in the old truck and drove to the dock. Now all that was left was to make the fifty yards down the length of the dock without getting shot. Both men knew that they were the targets, and the main reason there had not been an attack.

"Shaun, make a run down the dock with the truck. We'll never make it on foot," Henry told him.

"Slide down in the seat if you can and hold on to something!" Shaun stabbed the gas pedal to the floor, and the Chevrolet responded with a kick back through the carburetor and a fog of white smoke from the exhaust before it careened down the narrow dock.

Almost immediately, the front windshield shattered from small arms fire, and Shaun felt the left front tire trying to drag the steering over. He could see the ship and the men trying to return fire into the woods with their 9mm H&Ks, which were woefully lacking for this job. Nothing to do but try to keep it rolling for the next few yards now. The radiator was shot out and something had hit the top of the engine, but thankfully nothing had touched either man or the dog. Just a few more feet were left as the engine seized, and the old truck ground to a stop short of the gangway to the ship's deck. Henry had already opened his door and rolled out followed by Harry and Shaun as the shots from the wooded area continued to strike the truck body.

"You any good with that rifle, Henry?" Shaun indicated the old Remington that Henry held.

"It will depend on the rifle, I suppose. Why don't we find out?" Henry replied.

He crawled toward the front of the truck and peeked around to see if he could locate a target while they were firing, and then raised the rifle and took aim on a clump of shrubbery across the road. When he fired, a man stood straight up from behind the bushes and fell face forward, dropping his M-16.

"Nice shooting chief!" Shaun remarked, "Of course, it is only about fifty yards over there."

"There is always a critic! Are you ready to make the run for the ship?" Henry replied.

"Let's go!" Shaun responded and sprinted for the gangway with Henry and the Malamute close behind.

Henry heard the sodden impact of the bullet just a scant second before Shaun pitched head first off the gangway and onto the ship, his forward momentum bringing his body to rest against the bulkhead. Tuck was already moving quickly down the deck, crouching behind the relative shelter of the gunwale to get to Shaun. Henry rolled in behind the gunwale and then reached Shaun's right leg to pull him to safety.

"Tuck, I think he's gone, but I don't want that bunch to know," Henry said as Tuck joined them on the deck.

"Give me that rifle, Henry. I can help more with that than anything else right now. We need to get clear of this mess quickly," Tuck took the Remington and the box of shells before making a run for the wheelhouse and higher ground.

Henry pulled at Shaun's coat to reveal an exit hole in his chest the size of a quarter.

"At least they are using FMJ ammo, Shaun. If you can hear me, I'm going to get you out of here," he told the wounded man but got no response.

Suddenly there were two rapid fire shots from forward of his position that could have only come from the 30-06. Henry took a quick look over the rail and saw two men writhing on the ground at the end of the dock. The local tribal police showed up with their lights flashing, and a third man came from the woods with his hands raised in surrender. As Henry was looking, a loud klaxon sounded on the outboard side of the ship and Jerry stuck his head out of the wheelhouse to shout, "There is a Coast Guard cutter on the other side!" just as two Coast Guardsmen from the drug interdiction team came around the corner with their M-16s at the ready.

"This man needs a hospital immediately!" Henry shouted, "I don't care what it costs, I want his life saved."

One of the men kept Henry covered with his rifle while the other radioed the cutter. In a matter of seconds, there were two more seamen there with a Stokes stretcher which they loaded Shaun into and made for the cutter.

"You need to have your men stand down, sir," they told Henry.

"Help me up then," Henry replied.

"Tuck, stand down and bring the men down here!" he shouted to the wheelhouse.

Soon there were three men and a giant of sorts coming down the deck with their hands raised in surrender. It wouldn't do for a nervous youngster to shoot one of them after they had already survived an attack.

"You don't need the weapons, men," Henry told the two sailors that were staring at the men coming toward them, "The men that were trying to kill us held me captive on this ship in a coma until I managed to escape a couple of days ago. They have a cabin in the woods where all of the medical equipment is stored. These men are part of a team that my company put together to rescue me."

"The Lieutenant is sending a truck back for you. I'm supposed to deliver you to the station. He'll want to know about that cabin also," the young petty officer replied.

"I'll be happy to take him to it, but not before I check on my man," Henry told him.

As they were leaving the ship, a Coast Guard Bell 429 screamed down the harbor toward Vancouver Island.

"That would be your friend, I'm afraid, sir," the petty officer said to Henry, "We normally only use that one for medical emergencies."

"Let's go talk to the lieutenant and get this over with," was his reply.

Four hours later, with a good bit of persuasion from Constable Quincy Stuart of the RCMP, Henry and the men were free to go. The problem now was that the plane was sunk, and there was no other quick way off the island. Shaun had been flown by life flight to Vancouver General Hospital, and there had been no update on his condition.

"Men, I know the situation looks bleak, but I still have my bag of cash. I'm going to call around and see if we can get a ride out of here. One of you see if there is anyone here that will repair that DeHavilland and get it dropped at the airfield where Shaun rented it," Henry told them, "Darn shame that they don't like visitors enough to have a restaurant."

Two hours later, a large DeHavilland bearing the markings of the RCMP touched down in the harbor and taxied to the Coast Guard dock. Constable Stuart and one of his men got out and entered the area where Henry was waiting,

"Any word on Shaun's condition yet?" Quincy asked.

"Nothing yet, Constable. My men and I need to get back to Nanaimo and pick my plane up. I'll be going directly from there to the hospital in Vancouver once I find some decent clothes," Henry told him.

"Keep me posted on Shaun if you would, Mr. Albright, and if you would be so kind, give him this photo for me," Quincy handed him the picture of little Shaun, "I'll tell my pilot to drop you men off, and then return for me and the prisoners."

"Thank you, sir. I'll call as soon as I have word," Henry promised.

"One more thing, Mr. Albright, did Walter Grooms let on who had hired him to kill you and these men?" Quincy asked.

"Not directly, no, but one of his men did. My team will handle that matter in a few days. It would probably be better if you didn't know the details," Henry replied.

Quincy Stuart looked at him for a few seconds while he digested what had been told to him. This big man was certainly not what he seemed in the smelly fisherman's outfit, and might be a valuable asset in the future.

"I understand, sir. Well, good hunting then. Let's walk to the plane and get you on board." he replied.

CHAPTER SEVENTEEN

Bob Pike had gotten his group situated in the old three-bedroom parsonage. The refrigerator was stocked with basics, and the pantry had enough canned goods to feed the neighborhood. Hanna and her babies were in one bedroom with little Emily asleep and Michael Junior nursing. Maggie sat in the living room while Bob and Abigail cleaned the dinner dishes.

"Did you check to see if we had cable?" he asked Abigail.

"That is a funny question, Bob. You don't even like to watch television," she answered, "but it does appear to be hooked up."

"I thought we might get some news if anything major has happened," was all he replied.

They were interrupted by a knock on the front door, and everyone froze for a minute before Bob picked up the .45 and walked to the door with it behind his back.

"Can I help you?" he asked the older man who seemed startled by his presence.

"I'm sorry to trouble you, sir, but we thought that Pastor Shaun was home," the man answered.

"Pastor Shaun is away on family business, but we expect him back soon," Bob answered, "Is there anything that I can help you with?"

"My wife and I were wondering about tomorrow's service if it had been canceled or not?" he replied.

"Why, I can think of nothing better than to have a service in the morning. What time are they scheduled?" Bob asked.

"We normally get together for a bible study at nine o'clock with service at ten. I'm sorry, but are you a pastor?" the old man asked.

"Straight from Honduras to fill in for Shaun until he returns," Bob made up an answer.

"Wonderful! Pastor has mentioned the missionaries in Honduras many times. My wife will be delighted. By the way, my name is Elmer Brooks," he stretched out his hand.

Bob looked at the outstretched hand, and then put his left behind his back to take the pistol so that Elmer didn't have a heart attack.

"Bob Pike, Elmer. My wife is Abigail. We will see you at nine, so spread the word, and have a good evening," Bob shook his hand, and then ended the conversation by slowly shutting the door.

"Bob, are you sure we should do that?" Abigail asked from the kitchen doorway.

"Absolutely! Who hasn't benefited from a good church service? Besides, it is who we are now, isn't it?" he asked.

"I suppose so. I'd better tell the girls," she responded.

"And I'd better find the key to the church," Bob spoke to no one in general, "Lord, I hope you know what you're doing!"

Bob was in the church at seven thirty the next morning getting a feel for the place, and starting a pot of coffee in the small kitchen next to the fellowship room. Abigail showed up at eight thirty with a plate of cookies...just in case anyone actually showed up for the bible study, but Hanna and Maggie decided to stay out of sight in the parsonage. Abigail needn't have worried because, by eight forty-five, at least twenty people had gathered for the impromptu Sunday school and to meet the missionaries from Honduras.

Elmer and his wife Hazel were the leaders of the bible study which began late because of all the handshaking and questions.

Bob retired to a small pastor's study behind the sanctuary to prepare a sermon while Abigail stayed with the parishioners. At exactly nine fifty-five, Elmer dismissed the study and the troop filed into the sanctuary. Hazel took a seat at the piano and played softly until Bob opened the service with a prayer. After an hour of worship, sermon, and the inevitable passing of the plate, the service was ended with everyone congregating to talk to the missionaries that they had heard so much about.

Bob noticed the dark-haired woman in her forties that was advancing on Abigail even before she astounded them with a single question, "Is Hanna Tucker with you folks or did she stay in Miami?"

Abigail Pike just stared at her in disbelief as Bob suddenly appeared at her side and said, "Michael and Hanna Tucker died in a plane crash in New Mexico almost four years ago along with their daughter. Why would you ask such a question?"

The woman just smiled a cold smile and made her way to the door before turning and smiling again.

"Elmer, who is that woman?" Bob turned to Elmer and Hazel who had moved to the front entrance of the building.

"We've never seen her before, Bob. Maybe she dropped a visitor card in the offering. I'll go check," and they walked off to the church office.

"Abigail, I want you to quietly go out the back and get to the house. Tell Hanna what is going on," Bob told her.

"What is going on, dear?" Abigail looked stunned.

"We've been followed. Now, go! I'll clear the church and be there in a minute," he responded in an exasperated tone.

Elmer made his way back to Bob with a puzzled look on his face as he read what had been written on the visitor card. He handed the card to Bob and waited.

Bob took the card and read the writing, 'Hanna Tucker will die!'

"What does it mean, Bob?" Elmer asked.

"It means that someone named Hanna Tucker has a rough road ahead, apparently," Bob answered and put the card in his shirt pocket, "Elmer, if we are finished here, I need you to usher everyone out and lock up for me, Abigail isn't feeling well."

"Are we meeting tonight?" he asked.

"No, we are still recovering from our trip so tonight is canceled. We will certainly have our fellowship on Wednesday though," Bob smiled and walked to the back exit.

He entered the back door of the parsonage and looked around. Why Shaun had picked this cracker box of a building for a safe house was nagging him. It was time to make the phone call and find out. Bob retrieved the phone that had been found in the van and dialed the number that was entered in the speed dial. Half a world away a phone started ringing in a drawer at the Vancouver Hospital with no one to answer it.

Disappointed, Bob went to the living room where the rest of the refugees were sitting. Hanna was looking especially sullen, even for her mood swings after hearing the news from Abigail.

"Hanna, do you still have the phone that Tuck gave you?" he asked.

"It's in the bedroom, but I thought we weren't supposed to use it," she replied.

"Shaun isn't answering his, and this is kind of an emergency," he replied, "We need to talk to Tuck and see if he has any suggestions."

Hanna just nodded and walked to the room to retrieve her phone. Emily went to Bob and climbed in his lap, looking for a story from her new 'favorite' uncle.

"Maybe later, precious," he told her as her mother handed him the phone and took the little girl in her arms.

Bob hit the speed dial for Tuck and waited until it went into voice mail, which had not been set up.

"It looks like we are on our own," Bob spoke with frustration to the room, "I'm going back over to the church and look around. There was a reason for Shaun to move us here, and it certainly can't be this house!"

The congregation had left by the time he went back inside the two-story cinder block building through the back door, so Bob went straight to Shaun's office on the second floor. He looked at the two bookshelves that sat on each side wall but found nothing unusual. He then sat at the desk and began looking through the drawers with the hope of finding a solution to the dilemma that they now found themselves in. Shaun would have anticipated that they would be followed or that they wouldn't be able to communicate, so just what was the man's plan for this emergency? It was then that Bob's fingers brushed over a well-hidden piece of the drawer that moved when he touched it. He pressed a little harder and was rewarded with a slight clicking sound which came from the left side of the office near the floor to ceiling bookshelf. As he watched in amazement, the tall bookshelf retracted downward into the floor, revealing a steel pocket door set into the wall behind it.

Bob quickly got up from the desk and shut the office door before walking to the hidden door and pulling it open. Whatever that he had envisioned finding behind that door did nothing to suppress his surprise when it slid noiselessly open. Bob stepped through into a dark room and reached over to find a light switch. When the lights came on, he was standing on the top floor of a well-hidden, and apparently very well equipped safe house. It was time to collect the others and move in!

CHAPTER EIGHTEEN

The RCMP DeHavilland Beaver touched down near the Eagle Air dock. Amos had called ahead to explain the situation to Dixie, and she was waiting for the plane to taxi up when they arrived. He thought it best not to tell her about Shaun until after they had landed.

Dixie watched as they disembarked and grew noticeably agitated when Shaun did not get off the plane.

"Amos, where is Shaun?" she asked with a quaver in her voice.

Before he could answer, Henry spoke up, "Pardon me, Ma'am, I'm Henry Albright, Shaun's boss, and the object of this escapade."

Dixie sized him up quickly. Surely there was more to this big man than the filthy, fish smelling clothes that he had on.

"Dixie Renfroe, Mister Albright. Where is Shaun O'Brien and my plane?" She asked in a demanding tone.

"Your plane is being repaired, Dixie. We had some trouble and Shaun was shot. He has been airlifted to Vancouver Hospital by the Coast Guard, and we are on our way there now," he told her as straightforward as he could.

She stood looking at him for a minute with tears in her eyes before replying, "Mr. O'Brien and I had a deal. If he wrecked my plane, I would get to keep his," she answered.

"Dixie, I need to get into town, get rooms for my men and me, and then get a long, hot bath followed by some new clothes that don't have things crawling in them. Early tomorrow morning we need to fly to Vancouver to check on Shaun, and I would like to hire you for that flight in your new plane...if you would oblige us, of course," Henry told her.

Amos just stared at Henry before asking, "Boss, I'm standing right here. Don't you want me to fly the team out?"

"Amos, I need for you and my nephew to fly back to Miami and tend to your families. I am going to take Mike, Jerry, and Mister Hurricane with me after we make sure that Shaun is provided for," Henry replied, "The past week has taught me the importance of family, and I have selfishly kept you away from yours too many times."

Dixie spoke up, "You have a deal, Henry! I know of a very nice motel that we do business with that has a Jacuzzi in the master suites. Tomorrow, I'll fly you to Vancouver only because Shaun and I hit it off, and I have to know that he is going to be all right before we do any business after that."

"Good, now how about making a call so we can get ourselves cleaned up a bit?" Henry replied, "And see if you can arrange for a kennel for my dog if it wouldn't be too much trouble."

Dixie turned to the others that had been loading their gear in Shaun's rental, "Follow Henry and me to the motel. He is riding with me."

At ten o'clock the next morning the team, led by the huge 'Hurricane', descended on the Vancouver Hospital's intensive care unit like a phalanx of Praetorian guards escorting the Emperor Henry Albright, and with a determined Dixie Renfroe bringing up the rear. As they marched down the hall of the ICU unit to the nurse's station, they were met by a tired looking, slightly overweight nurse with the disposition of a bear.

"You people cannot be in here!" She growled as the men approached the desk area, "If you do not turn around and leave immediately, I will call security."

The large black man at the head of the group stepped aside to let Henry come forward and address the issue.

"Excuse me, ah...Nurse Hodges," Henry glanced at her name tag, "We have a friend in room 206 that we need to see. I also need for you to page his doctor and have him report here as soon as possible to update me on his prognosis."

"You can't bull your way in here, Sir. We have strict guidelines for gunshot victims and patients in ICU. What you want is not possible," She stepped back behind the desk and picked up the phone.

By this time several other nurses had gathered to gawk at what they thought might be a military takeover of the hospital, and one in particular just stood staring at Hurricane like he was the main course of a one-course meal. Before she could make the call, two men in suits came down the hall at a brisk walk, and the older of the two spoke to Henry.

"Mister Albright, I'm George Shuster, the hospital director. I got a call from Washington, DC regarding your man in 206, and I want you to know that you will have our full cooperation," he told Henry, "I hope our staff has not given you any trouble."

"Not at all, George. Nurse Hodges was just calling Mister O'Brien's physician for me, but if you could expedite his arrival, I would be most appreciative," Henry answered with a smile in the direction of Loretta Hodges, who looked as if she would burst a blood vessel at any moment.

"Anything that you need, sir, anything at all, and please come by my office on your way out," the administrator told him, extending his hand.

"I certainly will, George," Henry replied as he took the proffered hand, "Men, let's get to Shaun's room, and I would like for Dixie to have a couple of minutes before we all barge in."

The nurse that had been transfixed by Hurricane stepped forward and offered to take them to the room.

"My name is Kitty, and Mister O'Brien is in a very weak state," she offered as they walked down the hallway, "They didn't bring him up from surgery until almost four this morning, so don't expect him to be awake."

"I saw the wound before we had him transported, and it looked like the bullet came close to his heart. How much damage did it do?" Henry asked.

"I can't give you the details, sir, but I do know that he is the talk of the O.R. crew," she answered, "They are tossing the word 'miracle' around."

"Thank you very much, Nurse Kitty. You have been very helpful," Henry told her when they reached the room.

Kitty just gave him a smile and passed a piece of paper with her phone number on it to Hurricane, who seemed genuinely embarrassed by the attention. Mike and Jerry elbowed each other and gave him a look and big smiles while they waited for Dixie to see Shaun.

When they walked into the darkened room, they didn't notice the police officer that was seated somewhat behind the door when it swung open, but they noticed immediately the handcuffs that were restraining Shaun's left wrist to the bed rail.

"What in the hell have they got him shackled to the bed for?" an enraged Henry spoke loudly.

"Standard procedure for gunshot victims that get flown in here after a firefight on Canadian soil," came the response from the officer.

Henry turned to him and said bluntly, "I want those cuffs removed immediately, Officer. This man has immunity from prosecution here, and is no danger to anyone."

"I'm afraid that isn't going to happen. Just who are you anyway? I need to see some identification," the man answered, taking a belligerent tone and moving in Henry's direction.

Henry picked up the room phone and punched the button for the operator, "Yes, ma'am. I need for you to ring George Shuster for me, and tell him that Henry Albright is having trouble in room 206. Please do it now!"

As he was talking, the door had opened slowly and two large men slipped in the room unnoticed directly behind the officer, whose attention was focused on Henry, and the taser that he intended to use on the big man to bring him into compliance with what he thought was a lawful order.

When his left hand fell on an empty holster instead of the plastic grip of the weapon, there was a moment of confusion before he fell to the floor with his body racked with pain and convulsions.

"Nice shooting nephew!" Henry said to Tuck who still had his hand on the TASER.

"We thought you might need some help. Jerry and I will drag this one out so Dixie can spend some time with Shaun. How is he, anyway?" Tuck answered handing the TASER to Jerry.

"Well, he is still breathing, which is more than we hoped for yesterday," Henry said, "Let me give you a hand"

Just as they started to reach down for the officer a moan escaped his lips followed by the sound of a static discharge as another burst of electricity was released into the man's convulsing body.

"Jerry, what are you doing?" Tuck asked.

"He started to move, besides, he was going to Tase the boss," Jerry replied.

"Well, don't hit him again. He might have a heart attack," Henry told them as he dug for the keys to Shaun's handcuffs, "If this S.O.B. had Tased me, though, I would say to tape the trigger down, and let him enjoy the sensation until the battery drained."

"Unlock those things, Dixie. We'll be waiting outside," Henry pitched her the keys before they dragged the twitching and compliant cop into the hallway.

Then it was just the sound of the monitor beeping quietly as it displayed the vitals of the man that lay under the sheets of the hospital bed. Dixie removed his restraints, and then gently slid her hand under his as tears slid down her cheeks.

"Shaun, I don't know if you can hear me, but I need for you to get well," she told him in a whisper, "Something tells me that we are supposed to be together, and I won't accept you dying on me as an excuse."

She stood there for a few seconds before there was a small squeeze from the hand that she held. Dixie leaned over and gave Shaun a kiss on the forehead.

"Your boss is outside. I'm going to let them in now, but I'll be here when you really wake up," she squeezed his hand gently and went to the door.

Henry went in to the room alone and stayed for about five minutes talking quietly to Shaun. He knew that the injured man probably could hear him from his own near-death experiences.

"Shaun, we go back quite a long time, and I want you to know that I've considered you a friend and a valuable associate...a partner even. Now, I believe it is time for you to retire and enjoy the years that you have left, so I'm going to arrange that for you. I'll cover whatever expenses this hospital and your recovery accrue, plus a generous monthly pension. The reason that I am telling you this now is the young lady that just left the room. I'm also furloughing Tuck and Amos back to their families. We've lost too many years to this business, and, except for a special job here and there, when this threat against the family is dispensed with, I'm calling it quits. We'll talk again as soon as you are up and around," Henry finished and left the room.

"Ah...Mister Albright, how is the patient?" a smiling Chief Inspector Quincy Stuart asked when Henry stepped into the hallway, "I had a chat with the young policeman that your men roughed up. He isn't going to press charges, but I don't want this sort of thing happening again on our soil...agreed?"

"Absolutely, Chief Inspector. My men were just a little overzealous in protecting me from what they perceived as a threat. It won't happen again. Shaun is still under, but he seems to be able to hear. Did you want to see him?" Henry asked.

"Not right now. I'm going to be in the area for a few days, and I'll just pop in when Shaun can talk to me," he answered, "By the way, I have a bit of bad news to report. Your FBI man gave us the slip, I'm afraid. Our people are combing the island, but the chances of him being found there are very slim."

"He'll be making a run to Mexico to check in with his new employer. I'd like to be a fly on the wall for that meeting. Julius Salinas doesn't like failure, especially when he had poured money into the project," Henry told him.

"Salinas? That is who hired the hit on your family?" Quincy asked.

"That is our best guess, all things considered. We crossed swords with them several years ago down in Texas," Henry replied.

"Well, best of luck with that little project. If we can help, please let me know. Those drugs are killing our people too," he said, "I'll see you before the end of the week."

Henry waited until Quincy was out of earshot and then said, "Tuck, you and Amos go on in and see Shaun, but don't expect much. I want you on the next flight out. By the way, Tuck, have you talked to Hanna since you arrived up here?"

"My burner was on the plane when it sunk, so I haven't had a way to reach her. We were going to use Shaun's phone since Bob's number is in it, but we don't know where it is," Tuck answered.

"Look around the room when you go in and see if that phone is in there. You have a wife and two little ones that need to know that you care enough about them to keep in touch. Do I make myself clear, Tuck? Amos, that goes for you too," Henry told them.

Both men just nodded sheepishly and went into the room to tell Shaun goodbye.

"Jerry, I need for you and Mike to start the search for our elusive friend, starting with our contact in Tijuana. That is probably the most likely place for him to slip back in. He'll use the slackness of the California border security and just blend in. Where is Hurricane?" Henry asked.

"He was over at the nurse's station talking to the one named 'Kitty' the last we saw, Boss," Mike replied.

"I'll find him, you take Jerry and get us rooms for a few days...something like a Hampton Inn would be fine. Come back here and pick us up when you get settled, and we'll go get some lunch and make a few plans. Dixie, if you will allow me to take care of your accommodations while you're here, head out with those two and get settled. Shaun will be out of it for a few more hours so we have a little time to kill," Henry told them before heading for the nurse's station.

"You heard the man, boys. Let's get cracking!" Dixie said as she led the way out of the hospital.

CHAPTER NINETEEN

"Hang on Bob. I've got to see if there is any formula or diapers in the pantry. Michael Junior is running low, and I'm not making enough milk to keep him fed," Hanna said as she darted to the large, heavily stocked pantry.

"While Hanna is foraging, why don't you two head on over to the church office and wait for me. Be very careful when you step out of the house if there are any people out there. Anyone can be an enemy," Bob replied to the group.

Five minutes later, Hanna emerged from the kitchen area with a large bag of the necessary items, plus two packages of Pull-Ups for Emily in one arm, and holding little Michael in the other.

"I'm ready, Bob. Did Abigail and Maggie take Emily?" she asked.

"Yep. Let me take the baby or the bag," Bob offered.

A few minutes later, they were assembled at the desk in Shaun's office waiting for the surprise that Bob had promised. When the bookshelf slid down to reveal the steel door, all of the women gasped in amazement.

"You haven't see the good stuff yet," Bob said as he pulled the latch on the pocket door.

"My oh my, this is unbelievable!" Abigail exclaimed.

"Dad certainly has a flair, doesn't he?" Maggie laughed...a sound which seemed to lift the cloud from Hanna's countenance.

"Well, let's get in and lock it down. I have a feeling we'll be here for a few days. Abigail, how about taking stock of our provisions? I'm guessing that Shaun didn't shirk on those details either," Bob said as he locked everything up behind him.

The sound of the bookcase returning to its normal position was almost inaudible but very reassuring to him.

As Abigail headed down the stairs to the kitchen, and the others scouted the bedrooms on the upper floor with Emily running excitedly in the lead, the cell phone in Bob's pocket vibrated.

"Shaun, thank God you've called!" Bob answered excitedly.

"Hey Bob, it's Tuck. Are you all right?" Tuck asked.

"Tuck, where is Shaun? Did you find Henry?" Bob asked.

"Shaun is in the hospital in Vancouver, Bob, and Henry is fine. How is Hanna holding out?" Tuck asked.

"Tuck, we've got a problem here. We moved to the church when that trouble flared up in Miami, but someone came into the service today asking for Hanna Tucker. I found the safe room in the church and moved everyone over just a few minutes ago, but we have no fire power if these folks show up," Bob explained the situation.

"The situation is not as bleak as it might look, Bob. Amos and I are on the way back shortly, and there is enough ordinance in the back of the master bedroom closet to level a city block. Now, how about putting Hanna on so I can tell her the good news about Uncle Henry?" Tuck asked.

"Sure thing, Tuck. She is coming down the hallway now," Bob said as he handed the phone to Hanna.

"Michael Tucker, you had better have some good news for me," Hanna tried to sound annoyed.

"Hey Babe, we found Henry, Amos and I are on the way home," Tuck told her, "Shaun is shot up pretty badly, but they expect him to make a full recovery in a few weeks. He is at the Vancouver Hospital for now."

"That is terrible about Shaun, Tuck. I'll tell Maggie about it. He is going to be all right, though, isn't he?" Hanna asked.

"He'll be fine in a little while, besides, he has someone looking out for him up here," he told her.

"Someone? You mean like a woman?" Hanna was amazed.

"I mean. Listen, this thing is not over yet, but it will be shortly. Henry knows who is behind all of the trouble and is going to take care of it in a few days. We just have to keep our heads down until that happens," Tuck told her, "Listen, Hanna, I love you, and I'll be home in the morning, so just relax in the safe house. Amos wants to speak to Maggie."

Hanna handed the phone to Maggie who had heard them talking. She stood by her friend as she received both the bad news about her father and the good news that Amos was coming home with Tuck.

Maggie ended her call with, "I love you too, Amos."

Hanna noticed the tears starting in Maggie's eyes at the news of Shaun's injury, "He's going to be all right Maggie, and all of this will be over with soon."

"Hanna, I am so glad to hear the positive tone in your voice. Tuck must have given you some good news," she smiled.

"He did, and my daddy always told us that 'A good report brings health to the bones'. I feel healthier already!" Hanna hugged her, "Where did Bob run off too?"

"The last I saw him was when he ducked into the master bedroom down the hall here," Maggie replied.

When they caught up with Bob, he already had several M-4s, a case of loaded magazines, six grenades, and what looked like a dozen bricks of Semtex explosive laid out on the bed.

"That Shaun knows how to throw a party!" He laughed as they walked in, "Oh, I'm sorry about Shaun getting shot, Maggie. Tuck assured me that he was going to be fine," Bob felt embarrassed.

"That's okay, Bob. Amos told me that he has a girlfriend now, something that I've been praying for since Myrtle Beach. I also know that Henry Albright has furloughed, Amos, Tuck, and Shaun so they would slow down and spend more time with their families," Maggie told them.

"Michael didn't mention that part to me. Just wait until he gets back here." Hanna pouted.

"Well, that won't be until tomorrow sometime. In the meanwhile, we have to find out how Shaun intended to defend this place in case the bad guys show up before hand," Bob told them, "There has to be another way out downstairs, so I'm going to have a look around after I investigate that smell coming out of the kitchen."

"Emily, don't touch those grenades!" Hanna scolded as she picked up an M-4 and two magazines, "Let's go downstairs and see Abigail. She is probably making cookies from the smell coming up. Mags if you could take Emily, I've got to change Michael before his smell overpowers the cookies."

Maggie just smiled and picked up the little girl. She had a feeling that her time was coming soon.

Bob stopped by the kitchen to tell Abigail the latest news and was rewarded with a mixing spoon loaded with cookie dough, which he carried into what appeared to be a utility room at the far end of the large combination kitchen and dining room. It didn't take long for him to find another door that led into a tunnel that must have been built when the lot fill dirt was brought in to raise the driveway and the house above minor flood levels. Bob found a switch that turned on some dim lighting in the tunnel and then ventured in to find the other end.

The tunnel was made of three-foot diameter corrugated drain pipe with a twelve-inch flat grate on the bottom for a footpath. He stooped over for the entire fifty-foot distance of the tunnel until he came to another larger area with a short ladder in the end wall and a trapdoor in the overhead. Opening that door downward revealed a vertical room inside of a studded wall. Bob climbed up into the space and felt around for some way into the house. His effort was rewarded when a section of wall glided out almost effortlessly, and he was looking into the kitchen from behind where the refrigerator had been moments before.

Bob was ready to return to the church via the tunnel when reflected sunlight light lit up the kitchen through the living room windows. He walked cautiously into the next room and saw a black GMC Yukon pull up the drive and go around the house to the back entrance. Bob walked back through the kitchen and took the 1911 out of his waistband. He probably should have had one of the M-4s, but it hadn't seemed like the peace was going to be broken so soon.

As he peered cautiously out of the back kitchen window, he saw two familiar faces getting out of the Yukon. George and Tony made a very cautious approach to the back of the house with their weapons in a ready position. Bob opened the back door and motioned for them to hurry on in.

"Am I ever glad to see you men!" he exclaimed.

"Tuck called us a little while ago and told us to get up here. Our action didn't show down there, so we figured that the hit squad might have figured out our plan. Where is everyone?" Tony asked.

"Everyone is in the safe house as of a couple of hours ago. We had a visitor today that seemed to know that Hanna was going to be here," Bob replied.

"Okay, we'll stay in the house and try to get the jump on any attackers, if they show up. George and I can hold them off, and then evac down the tunnel to the safe house. We should be able to keep a small army at bay until Tuck gets back here in the morning," Tony told him.

"There are grenades and Semtex in the church that might come in handy. I don't think we can use them over there," Bob told him.

"Great! We'll follow you over and stock up. George is a wiz with things that go boom, so he probably will have a field day with the Semtex," Tony laughed as they followed Bob to the tunnel entrance. George came into the entrance last, moving the wall back into place as easily as it had slid out before retreating back down the tunnel to the safe house.

CHAPTER TWENTY

The meeting the next morning in the hotel lobby over a generous portion of the powdered eggs and sausage patties that headlined the 'Continental' breakfast was quiet, with every team member getting his final instructions from Henry Albright.

"Jerry, as soon as you and Mike find a hot trail, I'll follow with Hurricane and a pilot, if I can find one," Henry started.

Dixie kicked him under the table, "Easy Boss, I'm flying that Beechcraft out of here."

"Okay then, Hurricane, Dixie, and I will fly in as soon as the target is acquired. Don't make any moves on Grooms until we get there, I want to have a chat with him first...understood?" Henry asked.

"Yes, sir!" both Jerry and Mike spoke in unison.

"Hurricane, I want you packing while we are at the hospital, so don't let that nurse frisk you or anything," Henry told him, which caused the rest of the table to burst out laughing, "All right men, call when you arrive, and be careful! We will keep you posted on Shaun's condition. As soon as he is awake and out of the woods, we'll be ready to travel. You should have enough cash to grease the rails as needed, and the card is available also, but only for an emergency. I don't want a trail tying anything back to me."

"Do you think that Grooms will fly into San Diego?" Mike asked.

"I don't believe that he will fly at all. He had to leave the island by boat if the Mounties missed him, and my guess is that he is still on a boat. If that is the case, he will come ashore somewhere south of Tijuana...maybe a small fishing village. Spread a little green down there, and I think we will have some info that we can use in about three or four days," Henry told them, "Now get out of here. We've got things to do."

The group broke up with Jerry and Mike headed to the airport, and everyone else heading to the hospital for an update on Shaun. As they made their way to the ICU floor, Henry noticed what looked like additional security outside of the elevator and close to the nurse's station. Conspicuously absent was Nurse Hodges, but Kitty was sitting behind the desk.

"Good morning, Kitty. What is going on?" Henry asked quietly.

"These Mounties showed up about three this morning to provide security for Mister O'Brien," she answered, "Constable Stuart is in with him now."

"Is he awake?" Dixie asked nervously.

"Yes, Ma'am, Mister O'Brien has been trying to get out of bed since about two this morning." she replied.

"I'd like to see him," Dixie said to Henry.

"Okay, but let me go in first and see what Quincy is up too," he replied.

Dixie nodded in the affirmative, and Henry entered the room, "Good morning Quincy! How's our boy doing this morning?"

"Well, I thought that we would have to tie him to the bed again, but he's finally calmed down," Quincy replied with a laugh.

"Hello Henry, can you tell these folks that I need to get out of here?" Shaun asked weakly as Henry took his hand.

"No, I'm afraid that I won't do that, Shaun. In case you don't remember, you are officially retired, and on the dole," Henry replied with a smile, "So just relax and enjoy your stay. Besides, you lost your airplane to that lady from Eagle Air when you sunk hers...or don't you remember?"

"Retired? Henry, you can't do that to me, I've got too many responsibilities," Shaun tapered off.

"Not anymore. I want you to take some time and spend it with that young lady before you get too old and corrupted. Besides, I am throttling back the business as of next week, so you would have to collect unemployment instead of a pension anyway," Henry told him.

"Take the pension, Shaun. It will beat standing in line at the labor office every month," Quincy laughed, "By the way, Henry, I have some information that one of our contacts fed in this morning. That is why I ordered extra security on Shaun. You are going to want to act on this right away."

"What is it?" he asked.

"A tuna boat, the Lazy Lady, out of Seattle was spotted just South of Vancouver Island yesterday evening steaming south at a fairly high rate of speed considering the seas and such. Just after midnight, an SSB radio transmission was picked up from a vessel off Portland, Oregon, and was replied to from a station in Ensenada, Baja. We verified the locations by having our operators triangulate the signal," Quincy replied, "Of course, the transmission was a bit garbled at the frequency they were using, but the operators were able to enhance the message enough to determine that Ensenada is their destination."

"Then, that is our destination also, Constable. Now would be a good time to let Shaun talk to Dixie while I come up with a plan," Henry gave Shaun a thumbs-up sign before heading to the door.

"Henry, don't leave me here, for the love of God," Shaun begged.

"It is because of the love of God that I am, my friend. Mend up, and I'll bring Dixie back in a few days," Henry told him before he followed Quincy out of the room.

Once in the hallway and out of the range of listening ears, Quincy said, "I can't officially sanction this operation that you are heading up, Henry, but we can quietly give you intel on your quarry once you have a positive identity."

"I understand, Quincy, and I will protect any information that your people give us. Let me know how my small company can reciprocate," Henry responded.

"I checked into your 'small company', Henry, and if we ever need a war started or a government overthrown, I'll have you at the top of the list to call," Quincy laughed and shook Henry's hand before turning and walking out of the ward.

"Boss!" an urgent whisper came from an empty room to Henry's right.

Henry looked in and saw Hurricane standing over a uniformed man on the ground.

"What in the world are you doing, Hurricane? That man is a Mountie!" Henry spoke in a loud whisper.

"No sir, he isn't. Look at the shoes!" He replied.

Sure enough, the man on the ground was wearing a pair of dress shoes, right color, wrong style. Hurricane also pointed out that the uniform was slightly different also. Enough to pass a casual glance, but not an inspection from a professional.

Once they rolled him over, Henry retrieved the service weapon which had a threaded muzzle. They found the silencer taped to this leg under his sock.

"Good work, Hurricane! Now go to Shaun's room and send those Mounties down here. Stay with Shaun until we get this resolved," Henry ordered while dialing Quincy's cell, "Quincy, your security detail has been compromised."

"I'm still in the lobby. Are you secure?" came the response.

"So far. I've got your men coming to take the one we found into custody," Henry told him.

"I'm on the way," Quincy ended the call just as the two that had been guarding Shaun's room came running into the room where the imposter lay.

"Officers, this man is an imposter. Constable Stuart is on the way up, "Henry told them just as the man started moaning, "Well, that's a good sign. I thought my man had killed him."

Quincy came into the room right on the heels of his team and brought two more heavily armed men with him. They quickly got the dazed killer on his feet, and tie-wrapped like a hog for the market.

"I'll get what information that I can from him and get it to you, Henry," he said, "You two make a sweep of the hospital and make certain that this one was acting alone if he was. Your lives might depend on it!"

The two men that had come in with Quincy left the room and split up to check the ICU from room to room. The other two dragged the bound killer out of the area and down to a waiting transport van. As Henry and Quincy walked back to Shaun's room past the puzzled nurses standing at their station, an explanation of the event was just starting to come out of Quincy's mouth when the hospital quiet was shattered by first two shots, and then a volley of about fifteen rounds ripped from the two H&Ks that the Mounties were carrying.

"Call the main desk and have this facility locked down!" Quincy barked as he and Henry ran around the corner toward the sound of the gunfire.

At the far end of that hall, a man lay in a pool of his own blood while the two Mounties stripped his firearms from the body. Like his teammate, he was wearing street shoes and a uniform that looked as if it had come from the same costume shop.

"Good work men! There's a commendation is this, I'm certain," Quincy told them, "Have him picked up and then check the rest of the building."

He turned to Henry, "Get your team out of here. I'll handle the paperwork and the questions."

"Thanks, Quincy, I owe you," Henry shook his hand.

"Yes you do Yank, and I'll be collecting," he replied with a big grin, "Now get out of here!"

Henry went directly into Shaun's room, "There has been a change of plans, Dixie. We've got to go, and we have to go now! Hurricane, give your piece to Shaun. Shaun, Hurricane stopped a hit on me out there, but I want you to be careful and alert. Don't hesitate to shoot anybody that is not what he appears to be. Understood?"

"Hell, if that was the case, I should have shot you a long time ago!" Shaun replied with a weak grin, "Get out of here and take this blubbering female with you. A man can't get any rest with you people around anyway!"

Dixie leaned over and gave him a kiss, "You sure know how to sweet talk a girl, Mr. O'Brien. We'll see whose blubbering when I get back."

"Keep in touch with Tuck and Bob Pike for me, Shaun. We are on our way to Ensenada, Baja!" Henry told him as he ushered the others out of the room.

Shaun waved and waited for the door to close before inspecting the Colt Gold Cup 1911 that he now held in his hand with a big smile on his face.

CHAPTER TWENTY-ONE

Tony and George discussed their plans for defending against an attack over a simple throw together dinner that Bob and Abigail put together from various packages of frozen and dry foods that Shaun had stocked the pantry of both the parsonage and the church safe house with.

"George and I are going back over and set some booby traps just in case any unwelcome guests arrive here tonight...and I think they will. When they show, we will attempt to lure them into the house, and then make our retreat back down the tunnel to this location. Once here, we will get outside of the church and sweep for any survivors. When the authorities get here, we will be gone, so you all need to stay inside of this apartment until Tuck and Amos get here in the morning," Tony told them.

"Shouldn't we be helping you guys with the fighting?" Hanna asked.

"There isn't going to be any fighting, Hanna," George interjected, "We intend to kill everyone that shows, and then leave. Let it be a mystery to the authorities, although they will probably explain it away as a gas leak or some such."

"Well, I suppose the old place needed a makeover anyway," Bob tried to joke.

"Yeah, Shaun is going to be some kind of pissed that we blew his house up, but it might be a while before he gets back down here, from what Tuck told me. The boss is a very lucky man," Tony told them.

"Do you know exactly what happened to my father?" Maggie asked.

Both George and Tony shared a look that meant they had stuck their feet in their mouths.

Tony told her, "I'm sorry that I brought it up, but your dad was shot in the back, and the bullet nicked his heart on the way through. Tuck and Amos didn't tell you the particulars because they didn't want you to worry since it looks like he is going to be all right in a few weeks."

Maggie just clenched her teeth and thought about how many ways Amos was going to pay for this when he got home.

Thoroughly embarrassed by the slip of the lip, the men got up and made their way back to the tunnel with their sack of Semtex and two suppressed M-4s.

"Good luck to you all. We'll probably see you in Miami tomorrow afternoon," Tony said as he followed George into the tunnel.

"Now there go a couple of men that like their jobs just a little too much," Abigail told Bob.

"You might be right, Hon, but tonight I will thank God for them being here," he replied.

Baby Michael started crying in the living room where he had been sleeping while Emily watched one of her shows, so Hanna fixed a bottle of formula.

"Do you need some help, Hanna?" Maggie asked, "I need to keep my mind off of tonight."

"Sure, Maggie. I'm always glad for a little help with the kids. It will be nice to have a place to settle into after all of this moving and stuff, although I'm not sure how Michael is going to take the 'retirement', he is an adrenaline junkie after all," Hanna answered.

Everyone in the kitchen heard the anxiety in her voice and noticed that she had a shake in her hands as she worked. Bob and Abigail kept quiet but exchanged knowing glances. Hanna needed to be away from any of the nasty business that she and Tuck had gotten caught up in, and she also needed to restore aspects of her life that had been lost during the trauma of the past few years. Somehow, they were going to be there for this family that they had come to care for as their own.

All was quiet until shortly after midnight when Bob's cell phone buzzed with the simple text, "They're here!"

Bob woke Abigail, "It's happening right now, you probably should wake up the girls."

Abigail went to the other rooms and woke Hanna and Maggie, "Bob says that they are here."

Everybody moved quickly to retrieve either a pistol or one of the M-4s that were left, with Bob taking up a position at the inside of the upstairs entry point. Hanna went to the utility room to guard the tunnel entrance, while Maggie stayed in the room with the kids, covering the door with a model 500A Mossberg riot gun loaded with number four buck. Abigail nervously made coffee as they all waited for the surprise to play out next door.

In the house, Tony was watching from the front door windows when he saw two shadowy figures emerge from the darkness of the Palmetto grass lined driveway, and make their way quietly to the house where he and George had left the living room lights on and the TV blaring.

George came into the foyer, "There are at least four in the back, it is time to go."

They hurried to the refrigerator and made their way into the tunnel with George waiting at the entrance with the detonator in his hand. He had thought of putting the explosives on a timer but was afraid that a trip wire would alert some of the attackers to their danger. This way, he would have more in the noose when the trap was sprung, but at a little bit more danger to himself. Their only concern now was the corrugated pipe which might buckle when the charges were set off, but there were no options short of a firefight outside of the house.

Tony stopped halfway into the tunnel and waited for George to spring the trap, and he didn't have to wait long. The hit squad breached both front and back door simultaneously and swept their way past the empty bedrooms and into the living room. The last thing that their faces registered was the shock of finding the house empty.

When the Semtex detonated, the fridge slammed back into place and kept the brunt of the fireball and dust out of the tunnel, although George was stunned momentarily by the concussion. He felt Tony pulling at his arm and was surprised to find himself on his back with bleeding ears and a bloody nose. The two made their way to the church utility room where Hanna waited with her grenade and an M-4.

"Don't shoot Hanna, it's us!" Tony shouted, "Help me with George."

Hanna helped get George to the kitchen table, "You guys shook the church like an earthquake!"

"George always likes the big boom," Mike told her, "Don't you, Buddy?"

"I can't hear anything, Tony. Give me a minute," George responded loudly.

"I need to get outside and clean up before the cops get here. I don't think he is going to be any good with the shaking he got," Tony said to Bob.

"I'll come with you. George can stay here until Tuck gets here," Bob told him.

"You do know what I'm going to do, right?" Tony asked.

"Those men would have tried to kill me too, Tony. Let's get this done," Bob replied.

Abigail started to protest until she saw the determined look in Bob's eyes. She just hugged him, "Be careful."

"Okay, we are going out upstairs. Make sure that inside door is locked after we leave," Bob told them.

The two men left and made their way to what was left of the house which now looked like a pile of scrap lumber. Working quickly, Tony identified four bodies in the rubble, and Bob found two just inside of where the kitchen door would have been, one of whom was groaning. He reached down and took the balaclava off, then jumped back in surprise to discover the woman that had taunted him after the church service.

"This one is alive," he said to Tony as he came up.

Tony unceremoniously shot her in the head, "We need to go now, Bob. The danger is over with."

Still, in a bit of shock at the brutality of Tony's action, Bob followed him to the SUV that had been moved to the street. Lights were starting to come on all over the neighborhood and a siren sounded in the distance as they made their way to the interstate and back to Miami.

As soon as they were clear, Tony dug out his cell phone and made a call, "Everything is clear now. We need a cover story for the bodies."

"I was wondering how you intended to hide those," Bob said.

"Those were all cartel operatives, in case you hadn't guessed it, Bob. Worse than rabid dogs, which is why it doesn't bother me to put them down. The story on the news tomorrow will be something like a bunch of cartel terrorists attacked an empty parsonage by mistake and set off a gas explosion. Don't worry, we've had to deal with this type of scum before," Tony told him.

"Well, except for the one with the bullet hole in her head. We should have just covered her mouth and nose," Bob replied.

Tony just stared at him for a minute, "And here I was thinking that you might be a little squeamish being a pastor and all."

"I wasn't always a pastor, Tony. I was a game warden for twenty years up in South Carolina. There were a couple of times when I had to use deadly force, but it was never enjoyable to take another life, just necessary at the time," Bob replied.

The two rode in silence back to the parking garage.

CHAPTER TWENTY-TWO

After a stop in Miami to pick up a new set of IDs, change of clothes, Bob Pike, and one of the company's long wheelbase black Suburbans with all of the official markings of an FBI bomb investigator's vehicle, Michael Tucker, Amos Whitehorse, and Bob Pike drove to the church. As they made the turn onto the street where the parsonage used to be, Tuck had to give the siren a bleat to get the onlookers and the media out of the way. He pulled the rig up to the curb in front of the church and got out to greet one of the sheriff deputies that headed over to cut them off from access.

"I need to see some identification!" the deputy shout brusquely.

"Michael O'Hannon and Vincent Merriwether, FBI," Tuck replied as he stuck his ID in the deputy's face, "We are here to take a look at the damage."

The deputy appeared flustered, "Since when did this become an FBI investigation?"

"Since I got the call from Homeland to get my rear down here and take a look at it!" Tuck matched the deputy's tone, "Relax, nobody is stealing you boy's thunder, just making sure that this was not terrorist related. How about showing us around the area?"

"Yes, sir, just follow me," the man replied, "I just thought maybe we were being shoved out. Sorry about my tone."

"Nothing to be sorry about. We'd be upset if another group tried to build on our investigation also," Amos spoke up, "Have you identified the explosive that was used, yet?"

"We think that it was a gas leak that may have been set off during the break in, but one of the bodies has a hole in the head, so we are being cautious before making any announcement," the deputy replied.

"Well, another set of eyes won't hurt. Let's get up there and have a look. Have you found the people that lived here?" Tuck asked.

"No, we think that they might have been gone during the break in, but the church bus is still parked in the back of the wreckage with lots of blast damage," he replied.

They continued up the drive until the SUV was no longer in the line of sight. Bob had been well hidden behind the darkly tinted windows of the vehicle and waited for his opportunity to slip undetected around the church to the rear door. Further up the street, behind a tape police line barrier, he could see some of the people that made up the congregation, but Elmer and his wife were nowhere in sight. Tuck had parked the SUV just behind a huge clump of Palmetto grass that lined the church drive so Bob could exit the SUV unnoticed, but covering the twenty yards between the clump and the other side of the church was going to be tricky. Bob waited until all of the media seemed to be involved with statements from the congregation up the street, and then nonchalantly walked at a brisk clip to the far side of the church, around the side out of sight, and then to the back door, which he quickly unlocked and entered the building. Once inside, he breathed a sigh of relief before making the run to Shaun's office and triggering the latch for the bookshelf and the hidden door.

"Hey everybody, I'm up here, we need to hurry!" Bob shouted into the apartment.

"Coming, dear," he heard Abigail reply, "We'll be right out."

Soon everyone was in the office, and Bob closed the door to the apartment before leading them to the sanctuary to wait for the next phase of the plan.

"Emily, don't tell anyone about the apartment, Okay? That will be our secret," Hanna told her daughter.

"Can I tell Daddy?" she asked.

"Not until we are in the car, Honey," Hanna answered, "and act like you don't know Daddy or Uncle Amos, can you do that?"

"Yes Mommy, it will be like pretend, won't it?" Emily giggled.

"I'm afraid you are going to need a lot of therapy when you grow up, baby girl," Hanna told her quietly.

Bob made the call to Tuck, "We are as ready as we'll ever be."

"Unlock the front doors," Tuck replied with his back to the deputy, "Well, it looks like you people have been very thorough, Deputy. The only thing that I see that needs to be resolved is which one of the other dead people shot this woman. It almost looks like she set them up, and then tried to escape. By the way, did your people check out the church? We'd like to look in there before heading back."

"No, I haven't been over there yet, but it is not likely that they broke in there before this happened," he answered.

"Still, let's go over and give it a quick look before my partner and I head back," Tuck pressed.

"Okay, we can see if the front door is unlocked, otherwise we'll have to find someone in the crowd with a key. You know that there are always way too many keys floating around the congregations of these small churches," the deputy answered.

They climbed the stairs, and Amos turned the handle on the front door which opened easily into the church foyer.

"Anybody here?" he shouted.

"In here," came Bob's voice from the sanctuary, "Man are we glad you folks are here!"

The deputy stopped by Tuck and Amos to stare at the group in the sanctuary, "Have you people been in here all night?"

"Yes, sir, I'm Bob Pike, a visiting pastor from Honduras, and this is my wife, Abigail," Bob explained, "We were here with these folks having a prayer meeting last night when we heard the explosion next door. Honestly, we were too afraid to come out after reading about all of the gang violence in this part of America."

"I understand, Sir, but I am going to need statements from all of you before you can leave," the deputy told them.

Tuck stepped up and said, "Deputy, I think that these folk's testimonies could shed some light on this case. I'm going to take them with me and have our people debrief them in a less stressful environment. Don't worry, we'll have their statements and background histories sent back up by this afternoon."

"But...but...the sheriff won't agree to this," he argued.

"When I put in my report to Homeland how professional this investigation was handled by one of his men, he'll probably give you a raise!" Tuck laughed as Amos led the group to the vehicle.

"Okay, I suppose that will be fine. Just make sure to copy me on that report. Here's my card," came the replied.

Tuck smiled, shook the deputy's hand and put the card in his pocket.

Once in the car, Bob broke the tension, "We all need to repent for that bit of fabricating!"

"To quote a great preacher that I knew, 'God works in mysterious ways, Tuck'," Tuck replied with a grin.

"I know who that man was, Michael Tucker, and I'm certain that he would have frowned on us lying like that," Hanna chimed in.

Maggie looked at Amos and said, "Is there anything that you want to tell me, Honey? Like maybe your employment status?"

"Well, I was going to tell you when we got back in Miami, Maggie. Besides, I'm still on the payroll for a little while, just kind of in between jobs right now," he replied nervously.

"Truthfully, I've never been happier! Now I don't have to worry about getting a late night phone call to come pick up your body from somewhere," she smiled and gave him a kiss.

"How are the ears, George?" Bob asked.

"Ringing, Bob, but getting better. I appreciate you helping Tony last night," he replied, "I'm swearing off of explosives for a while after that."

"Well, I don't know how much help I was, but everything is all right now," he replied hopefully.

The young girl splashed playfully in the surf on a hot, sunny day in Myrtle Beach, watching her father and sisters sunbathing further away from the ocean. Suddenly the sky began to grow dark, and the waves seemed to grow to monstrous size as she heard her father cry out, "HANNA, HANNA!"

She tried to move back to the beach, but the water kept pulling her further and further away from the land until she could no longer see which direction the beach was. Panicking now, the girl kept shouting, "DADDY, DADDY," over and over, but nothing could be heard except the shrieking of the wind.

"Hanna, Hanna, wake up, you're having a bad dream!" Tuck shook his wife gently as he called to her.

"Michael? Oh, Michael, I've been having the most horrible dream over and over. My heart hurts from it," Hanna replied as she hugged her husband.

Tell me about it, Love," he asked.

"I really can't remember the details, Michael. It had something to do with Daddy, and I remember trying to swim," she responded, "Whatever it was about, it was very intense."

"How about if I fix us some hot chocolate? That will help us sleep," he offered.

"Having all of this stress off of me will do more, I promise. Do you think Uncle Henry will be able to fix this? If he can't, what happens to our children, Michael? Do you ever think about that?" Hanna questioned.

"You probably don't want to hear this, but I usually don't think about anything except what I have to do each day to get my job done. Whether that is to be a husband and father or do something for Shaun. Ever since we got involved in all of that nonsense with the cougar in Conway, I've never thought about anything long term," he replied, "It is just too much stress if you make plans just to have to abandon them."

"Are you such an adrenaline junkie that you don't want to be out of that espionage business? Exactly what are you planning on doing for a job now since Uncle Henry 'retired' you?" Hanna demanded.

"I haven't really given it much thought, Hanna, but it will not be something that keeps me gone for long periods. Maybe I could work as a hunting guide up in South Carolina. Bob told me that he ran into Tom Strongbow in Kentucky, and his hunting lodge is doing well. I might even get a pontoon boat and do flounder and trout fishing guide services at the beach," he told her, "Something will turn up, but first we have to get clear of the cartel and those trying to kill us."

"I changed my mind about the cocoa. Go make some and I'll check on the kids," Hanna answered, "We'll plan better at the kitchen table."

In another room, Amos and Maggie were also having trouble sleeping.

"Amos, I have been thinking that this might be a good time to go back to work," Maggie told him after sleep eluded them for several hours, "Maybe we could move to a small town back up in South Carolina, and I could do something local where we could be together at night."

"If you're worried about income, Maggie, don't be. I'm going to have a generous pension, plus we have quite a bit saved up in our nest egg," Amos replied, "Besides, I can always get a job dragging signs up and down the beach if needed."

"I'm just thinking that it might be time to expand our nest a bit, and if we do, I want our baby to have both of us home," she said.

"Baby? Do we want one right now?" Amos was stunned.

"I've just been helping with Hanna's children, and I'm feeling something, Darling. Wouldn't it be nice to have a little boy to teach your aviator skills to or a little girl for me to teach how not to take a load of crap off of men?" Maggie laughed.

"Can we discuss this over a cup of hot chocolate?" Amos asked.

"I was just thinking the same thing. Tuck and Hanna are already in the kitchen," she told him as she slipped on a robe and headed for the smell of chocolate and warm milk.

They were greeted in the kitchen by Hanna when they walked in, "Hey you two. You're just in time!"

"Like minds, huh?" Maggie replied, "What are you guys talking about?"

"Oh, just the normal stuff like, who are we gonna kill tomorrow, where are we gonna run afterward. Stuff like that." Hanna gave a laugh to show she wasn't serious.

"You had me going for a second, Hanna," Maggie replied, "Amos and I are going to discuss his retirement plans for raising a family, aren't we, Precious?"

Tuck just stood at the microwave heating the milk and shaking his head with a knowing smile on his face. Amos looked frightened.

"Well, it is a big step for an old fighter jock, you understand. One minute it's thrills and spills, the next minute, I'm changing diapers, and dragging a banner advertising sun tan lotion up the beach," he said.

"Well, at least you've got an idea. I'm thinking of some kind of guide service, anything that has some hunting and fishing in it. Junior is going to need to learn the swamps and backwaters if we go back to the beach, so I'll probably end up like Earl Johnson if Miss Fertile Myrtle has anything to say about it," he laughed.

Everybody laughed at that, and for the first time in weeks, Hanna felt the sunshine start peeking through the depression that had been gripping her. It was finally looking like everything was going to be all right. Well, at least there appeared to be a glimmer of light showing at the other end of the long tunnel. They were soon joined by Bob and Abigail who had the same idea about hot chocolate, and the three couples talked until well into the wee morning hours. The little party finally broke up when Michael Junior cried out for attention from the bedroom.

"Duty calls, folks," Hanna announced as she started out of the room.

"I'll help, Hanna. I need all of the practice that I can get," Maggie followed behind.

"Darn, I told Tony that I'd come down and relieve him about four am. I've got to hustle," Tuck announced.

"I'll come with you. Who knows when we will have any excitement in our lives again?" Amos told him as they left the kitchen.

"What do you think, Abbie?" Bob reached across the island table and squeezed her hand.

"I think that barring any more misery, Hanna is going to be all right, Bob. What do you want to do with the rest of our lives?" she asked.

"Hmmm... maybe we should pray about it and see what God wants us to do. There is the mission in Honduras that never really seemed to fit, a church up the road that will need an interim pastor until Shaun recovers, although I have the idea that he isn't coming back anytime soon, and those kids are going to need some godly influence in their lives as they make this difficult transition from fugitives to living in a subdued environment again," Bob told her, "but I think I just spoke what God has on His mind about the situation."

"Prayer is always a good option, Bob. Drink your cocoa so we can go back to bed," Abigail replied with a tired smile.

CHAPTER TWENTY-THREE

"Better call the boss, Mike. The Lazy Lady is just entering the harbor," Jerry said as he scanned the harbor entrance with a set of old Leupold 9x35 Porros Binoculars that he picked up from a pawn shop in San Diego.

"Roger that, Jerry. Keep an eye on her while I get him on the horn," Mike took a cell phone out and made a call to Henry's number.

"Albright," came the one-word answer.

"Hey Boss, the boat is coming in now, and looks like maybe thirty minutes to the dock," Mike told him.

"Get in position Mike. I want this clean and quiet," Henry ordered.

"Yes Sir, clean and quiet it is," Mike acknowledged the order and ended the call, "We're on, and the boss said 'clean and quiet'. Do we know any other way?"

Jerry laughed and the small fishing boat that they had chartered moved past the Lazy Lady in a way that would put them on the dock a few minutes before she berthed. Henry speculated that the ship's crew would be on the cartel payroll and very dangerous to approach. The plan was to follow Walter Grooms until he was alone, grab him, and then convince him to tell them where Julius Salinas was staying. Simple enough to plan, another thing to execute.

"I wish Tuck was here with us. We could use that spider sense thing that he has going for him." Jerry said.

The eighty-five-foot aluminum hull tuna boat, The Lazy Lady, berthed about fifty feet down the pier from where Jerry and Mike sat on the old wooden hulled forty-two footer that had seen much better days. Both men had adopted the look and smell of fishermen that had been on the water several days, and the short, stocky Mexican fisherman that captained the boat lent authenticity to their disguise. To the casual onlooker, these were hard luck fishermen, but a closer inspection would reveal something far more lethal.

The first two men off the Lazy Lady were obviously deck hands from the white rubber deck boots and rubber rain gear bottoms they wore. Several others in street clothes came by next without more than a look of disdain for the crew on the old boat.

"Here he comes, Mike," Jerry said quietly as a man in a tropical suit stepped off the tuna boat.

"Yeah, but take a gander up the dock. We've got company," Mike said, "Do you recognize the guy in all of the jewelry, Manny?"

Manny Hernandez replied, "That is Julius Salinas, and I think we might have a little trouble."

"This might blow the plan guys, be ready for anything. Manny, how about getting this old bucket fired up...just in case we need to make a break for it."

Manny fired the old 671 diesel and waited. Julius Salinas was being escorted by two bodyguards, but Mike was sure there were more on the landing. When they were about twenty yards from the boat, Salinas held up a ringed hand to signal the bodyguards to wait, and then continued toward Walter Grooms who had stopped right beside Jerry.

Manny stood behind the wheel of the old boat in the half cabin and opened the front windows as he slid the concealed suppressed M-4 across the dash and waited.

Jerry turned to Mike, "No time like the present."

Mike nodded and signaled Manny. Almost in unison, the two bodyguards dropped from Manny's head shot wounds, and Julius Salinas fell to the dock with both knees shot through. Walter Grooms staggered backward from the multiple rounds that he took to the chest from Mike and fell into the harbor. Mike and Jerry jumped to the dock and managed to drag Salinas back and dump him unceremoniously into the shallow deck box packed with ice and bait.

As small arms fire started ranging the boat, Jerry shouted, "HIT IT, MANNY!"

Mike threw off the lines with numerous rounds whizzing past his head, and they managed to get into the harbor without being hit more than a dozen times.

Mike sank down behind the gunwale and called Henry, "Change of plans, Boss! We have Salinas, and we need some help!"

"Tell Jerry to head for open water. If that old tub makes it without being sunk, we'll pick you up there." Henry told him, "Is Julius dead?"

"Not yet. I shot his legs out from under him, and we have him on ice...literally," Mike reported.

"I love you guys! Now get your asses out of there. I'm on the way!" Henry roared into the phone.

"Henry says he loves us, Jerry!" Mike shouted over the roar of the old diesel.

"I hope he has a contingency for this or we are going to be dead in a few minutes!" Jerry shouted back, "Hey Manny, does this thing have any more speed?"

"Señor Jerry, my cousin's boat is used in the family business. Of course, it has more speed!" Manny shouted back with a grin.

He pulled a hidden pin that had prevented the throttle from being pushed completely forward, and the old boat seemed to jump ahead as the turbocharger on the 671TI started whining. Now they just needed to make it to the breakwater before something much faster could run them down, and they would be relatively safe in the ocean that had been chopped up by a late afternoon breeze.

As luck would have it, and it usually does when it is about to run out, Mike spotted the fifty-two foot, bright red Cigarette hull that belonged to Julius Salinas as it came out of the harbor at more than seventy miles an hour. They weren't going to be able to outrun this one even if the ocean got up to five feet or more.

"Take the lid off the fish box, Mike," Jerry shouted," I've got a plan."

"In case you need reminding, your last plan got us out here," Mike told him as he took the lid off.

"Yeah, yeah, help me get him up," Jerry ordered, and they pulled the screaming Julius to a seated position on the edge of the box.

"Pull the throttle back, Manny. We can't outrun them anyway," he told him as both he and Mike held their Berettas to the head of one of the most powerful and most ruthless men in Mexico.

Manny took the boat out of gear and propped up on the side of the cabin with his M-4 trained on the Cigarette that was fast approaching. Just as it came within a hundred yards, Mike's cell phone rang.

"Hello, Henry. We are a little busy at the moment," Mike tried to sound light hearted.

"Mike, I'm on the Cigarette! When we get alongside, load Salinas in," Henry told him.

"It's okay men, that's the Boss!" Mike shouted with relief.

When the sleek machine thundered up alongside with its three, five hundred cubic inch Chevrolet engines barking at idle, Mike and Jerry dragged Julius screaming in pain to the side where a big hand reached over and threw him into the boat.

"Manny, can you make another port?" Henry shouted.

"Yes, Sir, Mister Albright. My cousin has a little place to hide not too far to the north," Manny replied.

"Here's the payment that I promised with a bonus, and we appreciate your help," Henry said as he handed over a pouch of money.

"I was glad to help get this trash off the streets. Vaya con Dios, my friends. See you in Texas sometime!" Manny threw off the line and eased the boat away with a wave of his hand.

"You had us worried for a minute, Boss. What are we going to do with him?" Jerry asked.

"His body I am going to send to the authorities. His head is coming with us," Henry replied with a coldness that his men had never seen, "Hurricane, take us to the Naval Air Station in San Diego. I'll have Dixie get the plane warmed up."

Where to next, Henry?" Mike shouted as Hurricane pushed the throttles up, and the big Chevrolet engines roared through the unmuffled exhausts.

"I think that we need to take a trip to Acapulco, boys. How about a little R&R?" Henry laughed loudly over the thundering roar of eighteen hundred horsepower bashing through the ocean toward San Diego.

As the boat crashed through the marginal seas, eating up the roughly seventy-mile trip to the Naval Air Station on North Island where Henry had pulled some strings to allow Dixie to land the Beechcraft, He dragged Julius Salinas to the stern of the boat where the ride was not as choppy.

"Julius, my name is Henry Albright. I'm the man that you sent your people to kidnap. Now that didn't turn out well for them or you, did it?" Henry asked.

"I'll have you killed, you fat piece of..." the thought was interrupted by Henry sticking a seven-inch blade into Julius' throat, and severing the carotid artery.

"Now you are starting to understand, amigo. I can see it in your eyes," Henry told the rapidly dying former drug kingpin and psychotic killer.

When the blood quit pumping from the throat wound, Henry quickly took the head from the body and signaled Jerry to bring the body bag that they had brought along for the occasion. Jerry and Mike made short work of getting Julius' remains in the bag, while Henry slipped the head into a plastic sack and placed it in the forepeak of the boat on one of the V-berths.

"How are we going to explain that body to the authorities, Boss?" Jerry asked.

"Simple enough, his second in command, Javier Ortega, had him killed and kept the head for a souvenir. We'll start that rumor up here with the authorities, and get down to Acapulco before the rumor mill has time to work," Henry told him, "Dixie is supposed to have shopped for a gift box while we were busy. We'll see how she did."

Two hours later the vibrant red Cigarette hull was moored at the Naval Air dock with several official cars and an ambulance parked in front of it. Henry was talking to a Navy Commander as the base medical personnel loaded the body bag into the ambulance. After a short conversation, the Commander shook Henry's hand and left the scene.

"Come on, men, we've got a plane to catch. By the way, Hurricane, can you retrieve my bag from the berth, please?" Henry asked.

"Certainly Boss," Hurricane answered with a look of disgust on his face as he gingerly handed the retrieved bag containing the late Julius Salinas' head, "Those things just give me the creeps with the eyes staring up at you."

"I'm hoping it will have the same effect on Javier. If it is any help, killing this guy by cutting his throat was a merciful act considering what he has done to hundreds of his countrymen and untold addicts in our country," Henry told him, "Don't dwell on it. I need all of you sharp when we confront Javier."

A taxi pulled up to the dock, and the three men got in with Henry's trophy.

"Take us to the airfield, please," Henry told the driver.

"What about the boat," Hurricane asked.

"The Coast Guard will probably be running interdiction patrols in it pretty soon. They like the psychological effect of using a drug lord's equipment when they can," Henry answered.

"They'll be singing ballads about this operation after today, Boss," Hurricane told him.

"Nobody can ever know we were here," Henry replied quietly, "Pull over to the Beechcraft, driver."

Dixie greeted the men by waving from the door of the twin-engined plane while Henry tipped the cabbie generously.

"Hey Boss, I went shopping for something to put the present in that you talked about. There wasn't anything around except for some very nice yellow acorn baskets with a green top for a lid. I got a deal on an even dozen," Dixie told him.

"I'm hoping this is a one-time deal, Dixie. What am I going to do with eleven more baskets?" Henry replied.

"You'll think of something...now we need to rock if you want me to get you there before dark," she replied.

They soon were wheels up and headed for Acapulco where it was rumored that Javier Ortega could be found. The rumors seemed to be substantiated by the number of headless corpses that had been found recently around the sprawling city, something of a trademark of Javier's management style. There was even speculation north of the border that the beheadings were a direct result of the Muslim schooling that had been establishing footholds in the poorer sections of Mexico as the influence of the Catholic church and their schools had been waning.

The Beechcraft touched down about an hour before the sunset in Acapulco, and Henry briefed Dixie on the procedure for out of country flights.

"We haven't had much time to talk about this, Dixie, but I am assuming that your paperwork is current. Is it?" He asked.

I've got everything that I'll need to satisfy the Mexicans. Is the plane paperwork all here? You know that they are going to want to see everything," she answered.

"This one has been across Mexico before. They tried to shoot it down back then," Henry laughed, "Relax, the Airport Commandant is a friend of mine, and he talks the kind of language that doesn't need an interpreter. There is a room in your name at the Bambaddha. Check in there and wait for us to get back. We'll have an operational meeting tonight over dinner, so keep close to the airport, and keep your cell phone on. When we finish tomorrow, we are going to need to leave pretty quickly."

"Everything will be ready, Boss. I hope your friend likes his present," Dixie told him but had no idea what Henry was carrying in the box.

"I'm certain that he will find it riveting, Dixie. The acorn basket was a nice touch, by the way," Henry told her and then turned to the men, "Let's go, men. Make sure that you have the passports that I gave you handy, and don't take any armament with you. I've made arrangements to pick up 'supplies' when we get out of the airport."

The three men each gripped their overnight bags with a change of clothes and followed Henry off the plane to a waiting official vehicle that carried them to the commandant's office and Mexican customs. Once there, Henry was greeted by a well-dressed gentleman that obviously held him in some regard.

"Henry Albright! Imagine my surprise to hear that you would be visiting me today. I've left my calendar open for you and your men," he said with a large grin.

"Raul, it is good to see you after all this time," Henry shook the man's hand and accepted the invitation to sit.

"Well, Henry, I know you well enough to get right to the point. What can I help you with on this trip?" Raul asked, leaning forward and resting his elbows on the desk.

"I've got some business here in Acapulco that might entail having to leave on a short notice. Can you help me out with that?" he replied.

"My friend, we go way back, and I believe you put it most eloquently when you told me that we spoke the same language on one of your visits. Are you going to speak to me now?" Raul had what looked like a small expectant smile on his lips.

Henry turned in the chair slightly, and reached back for a briefcase that Hurricane was carrying, "I think that this might speak loudly enough to be heard, Raul."

Raul Garcia flipped the latches on the briefcase and peered inside. Even a man as jaded as he was could be surprised at the generosity of Henry Albright, as his face showed.

"Consider everything handled my friend. Let me make a call to our security and get you and your men clearance to leave the airport, and if you need anything else, just give me a call. There is a young lady in the outer office that will stamp your visas. Have a nice visit to our lovely city," Raul stood to indicate that the meeting was concluded and Henry shook his hand. Since the language of criminals had been exchanged, there was no need for further conversation. The party in Acapulco was on!

CHAPTER TWENTY-FOUR

Tuck and Amos had relieved two of the men that were reinforcing Tony and George's effort to keep the ground floor of the building secure. About two hours into their watch, Amos called over to Tuck.

"Hey Tuck, take a look at those two men in the old pickup just down the block from us. Isn't that an RPG the tall one is carrying or are my eyes playing tricks?" he asked.

"It sure looks like the launcher anyway. Go get Tony," Tuck replied as he steadied up the Remington on the catwalk rail and turned the magnification up on the Leupold scope.

"Whatcha got, Tuck?" Tony asked as he came running up below the catwalk.

"Better get everybody up, Tony. We are getting ready to get hit!" Tuck exclaimed.

"Have they loaded it yet?" Amos asked.

"No. I'm guessing that they are waiting for some reinforcements to arrive. If they had that thing loaded, I'd go ahead and take a shot on the carrier, but shooting him while he is holding an empty tube would probably be seen as murder here in Miami." Tuck told him without taking his eyes off the two men with the launcher.

"There is more movement about two hundred yards down the street on this other end!" George told them.

The other men started manning the defensive platform while Tony moved two SUVs in sideways to the roll-up door to block any entrance to the building if the door was breached. Tuck concentrated on the pick up where the first two had hunkered down. A plan was forming in his mind now that it was certain these guys were going to attack. He had a 168-grain hollow point chambered in the .308, now he eased the safety to the off position and waited for the 'rocket man' to make his move.

"Tony, call the Miami PD and tell them that a group of terrorists is getting ready to blow up the Trade Winds building. That will give us probable cause when I light this guy up," Tuck said to Tony.

"I'm on it!" he replied and made the call.

Tuck watched the two stand up from behind the truck with a grenade now loaded in the launcher.

"RPG 7!" he shouted and took steady aim on the grenade itself.

Tuck had about five seconds as the trigger man, who obviously didn't realize he had been seen, took his time to aim the launcher at the steel roll-up door. His loader had stepped back slightly to the man's left side, and out of the way of the back blast from the tube. Tuck waited until the grenade was just on target and squeezed off his shot, which made impact directly on the side of the grenade, violently slamming the launcher back to the trigger man's right and directing the grenade straight down the street where the other attackers had parked. The surprised attacker jerked the trigger igniting the gunpowder launching charge which rushed out the back of the tube, hitting the hapless loader directly in the face. The grenade blasted out of the tube about ten yards before the rocket motor started, and then flew erratically down the street before striking the pavement short of the first SUV and skipping like a stone on a pond surface up under the car and detonating directly in front of the fuel tank. The resulting explosion ruptured the polypropylene tank and vaporized the twenty gallons of gasoline in a huge fireball that violently consumed the two men that had been standing directly behind the vehicle, and catching the second car on fire as its occupants tried desperately to escape the unexpected inferno.

"Nice shooting, Tuck!" Amos slapped him on the back.

"Hold your fire everyone. I hear the locals coming into the neighborhood," Tony called out, "Nice call on not killing the rocket man, Tuck. He's going to have a hard time explaining what just happened!"

"I'm a little confused myself, Tony. I thought for sure that thing would blow up and kill the two on this end. That has to be some kind of 'Divine' intervention!" Tuck replied before turning to the others, "Okay men, back to the tunnel with the weapons. Amos and I will handle the police."

Tuck phone rang, "Tuck here, Bob."

"We heard the explosion up here, and the girls are worried," Bob told him.

"Tell them that it looks like two rival gangs picked our street to fight it out on. The police are outside now," Tuck told him, "I'm going out and have a word with them."

"Give me an update when you finish," Bob ended the call.

Tuck waited until all of the men but Amos were gone from the garage, and then stepped out through the entry to the side of the roll-up. He waved to what looked like the officer in charge to get his attention. The man gave some orders to one of the others and then came across the street to Tuck.

"Boy am I glad to see you, Officer!" Tuck said, trying to sound relieved.

"Are you the one that called this in?" he asked.

"Yes, Sir. I'm Ron Greene, Shaun O'Brien's assistant here at Trade Winds," Tuck said as he presented his ID.

"What were you doing up at this hour Mr. Greene?" The officer asked.

"Just a last minute check to make sure we were ready for a shipment that is coming in tomorrow, sir. I happened to look out that window over there and saw that guy pointing his rocket thing at those people down there. The next thing I knew, he had fired and the cars down there blew up," Tuck tried to sound as distressed at the violence as he could.

"Okay, Mister Greene. I'll need you to come by the station tomorrow and make a statement. Thank you for being a concerned citizen," the cop shook his hand and went back to his car just as the firefighters showed up with the rescue equipment.

Amos was waiting for him inside the door, "My, you sounded positively sweet out there, Tuck."

"I did, didn't I? Must be from hanging around a flyboy too long," Tuck responded with a laugh, "How about getting Tony to send up a couple to relieve us. I need some sleep."

"Sounds good to me. I'll see you upstairs," Amos replied and went to the intercom to signal Tony, "Hey Tony, we're heading up. Can you send two up to replace us?"

"On the way. Tell Tuck to hang around for a second. I need to talk to him," Tony told him.

"Hey Tuck, Tony wants to talk to you before you head up. I'm leaving," Amos said.

"Okay, I've got to get in touch with Henry anyway," Tuck replied.

Tony came up with George and walked over to Tuck, "I'm worried Chief. If those guys are serious enough to break out the RPGs, I don't think that we can hold them here. Have you got a backup plan?"

"With the wipeout they took tonight, I would be very surprised if anything else happened before tomorrow evening. I'm going to get in touch with Henry in a few minutes to see if they've made any progress. If we have to, there is always Shaun's crew boat. We could put out in that and wait it out in the ocean, I suppose," Tuck responded.

"I get sea sick so let's hope the big boss has a breakthrough," Tony laughed and slapped Tuck on the back, "That was a helluva lucky shot, Tuck. No wonder everybody saw the halo around you in Afghanistan."

"Long time ago, Tony. I'll see you later in the morning," Tuck replied and took the elevator up to the apartment.

CHAPTER TWENTY-FIVE

Henry was his old relaxed self when he joined Dixie, Mike, Jerry, and Hurricane for a light breakfast in the hotel restaurant the next morning, a side of the old man that they had never seen. Of course, two of the members of the team had never seen him at all until he showed up dressed in old oilskins and reeking of fish and body odor...not all of it his.

"Jerry, I want you to take the team into the streets and find the most likely spot to run into Javier Ortega. Dixie and I've got some shopping to do, so we'll catch up as soon as you send word. Rent an inconspicuous vehicle and try not to attract too much attention," Henry gave them their marching orders.

"We're on it, Boss. Are we going to be here another night?" Jerry asked.

"I'm thinking not, so check out after breakfast. If something comes up, we can always get another room," Henry replied, "Dixie, have you talked to Shaun?"

"This morning, Henry. He called me very early and said that he wants out of that 'damned' hospital. His words, not mine. I think he is going to make it," she answered.

Henry laughed, "He'll thank me when this is over...trust me."

Jerry just looked at Mike and rolled his eyes.

"I saw that!" Henry told him, but smiled, "You two know as well as I do that if we let Shaun out of the hospital, he would be down here trying to help and probably get shot again."

They all agreed with a laugh, and Henry left with Dixie to catch a cab and get some shopping done. By the time that they were 'properly outfitted' in Henry's terms, Dixie looked for all the world like an aviatrix from the nineteen thirties. Henry insisted that if she was going to fly for him, she had to at least look the part. Dixie thought he was being a little chauvinistic, but deep down, she liked the attention and the clothes, and couldn't wait to show off her new wardrobe to Shaun when they got back.

Just after Henry finished his shopping and had decided to wear the outfit that he had bribed the tailor to rush alterations on, Jerry called with the news.

"Boss, we found him. Javier and his boys are at the Copa Cabana. From what we've been able to gather, they've been pretty busy in a little turf war down here. Your gift will be in style...if you know what I mean," Jerry reported.

"That is good news, Jerry. Now bring the rental and pick us up. As soon as we can find a limo, Dixie will take the rental back to the airport and get the plane ready. That is if she can fit her new clothes in," Henry laughed.

Dixie spoke loudly enough for them to hear over the phone, "Oh, I'm going to get them in there, even if one of you has to fly home commercial!"

By the time that Jerry made his way through traffic, Henry had rented a light tan Lincoln limousine with a driver and had him waiting at the shopping center.

"Wow, Boss! The car matches your suit!" Mike laughed, "The hat is a nice touch too."

"Thanks, Mike. I told Dixie that the first one of you that paid me a compliment would get a raise," Henry said with a wink in her direction.

Mike gave Jerry an elbow in the ribs in an "I'm the man" statement which Jerry tried to ignore.

"Okay men, are we ready to do this like we rehearsed?" Henry asked, and when they gave him the affirmative, "Let's go get him. Dixie, we'll call when it is over. If you don't hear from us before dark, get the plane out of here and go back to Vancouver. Shaun will know what to do, understand?"

"I understand, Henry, but the plane will be ready when you call," she replied with a smile.

The lounge at the Acapulco Copa Cabana was spaciously decorated with woven cane furniture in a laid back beach motif that included a lounge chair big enough to hold two people. Today, there was a young man in expensive beach attire reclining with an attractive Latino woman that had more jewelry than clothes adorning her body. When the extremely wide man in the light tan suit, silk shirt, Gucci loafers, and Panama hat walked into the room accompanied by three bodyguards, all eyes in the room followed him, and all conversation stopped.

The suddenly silenced room made Javier Ortega take his attention off the beautiful woman that he was sharing the lounge chair with, and turn his head in Henry's direction, just as four of his bodyguards rushed to block Henry and his entourage from approaching the center of the lounge where Javier was now watching.

As one of the men reached out to impede Henry's stroll, a massive hand that was attached to an arm three times a normal person's size, caught the extended fingers of Javier's bodyguard and broke them with an audible crack that was heard across the room. Hurricane stepped back behind Henry with a stoic look as if nothing had happened while Mike and Jerry moved to the left and right of Henry in defensive positions, although neither of them had drawn a weapon. Coupled with the vision of the grizzly bear in a tan suit, the small force was impressive, even to the professionals that made up Javier's guard.

Henry held up his right hand and spoke, "Señor Ortega, I wish you no harm. My men are standing down."

"You've got some nerve to approach me like this, Gringo, but I like nerve. Let my men check you for weapons before we talk," Javier replied.

Henry raised both arms so that one of the others with two good hands could frisk him. When the man was finished, Javier waved him forward. As Henry walked the few feet that separated them, he heard the unmistakable sound of rounds being racked into various semi-auto pistols and hoped that these folks weren't as trigger happy as they seemed. Who was he kidding? Just yesterday, the local papers were filled with stories of brutal beheadings and mass graves in the area, and this group was getting all of the credit for them.

"Sit down Amigo and tell me what your business with me is," Javier seemed to be jeering at Henry.

"I'll cut to the chase then. What if I told you that I could give you instant control of your organization?" Henry asked him.

"You are a very loco gringo if you think that, Señor. Our leader would have you killed in about three seconds if he heard you say this to me," Javier nervously replied, trying to force a smile of disbelief. If one of his men went to Julius with this report, then Javier's head would likely be in a ditch by morning.

"For the sake of argument, let's say that I could convince Julius Salinas to turn over control of this business to you, what would it be worth?" Henry pressed him.

Javier seemed to become aware of the woman sitting next to him for the first time since Henry came in, "¡Deja! (Leave!)" He shouted roughly as he shoved her away.

"You could just about name your price, although what you are talking about is foolishness. I will have you killed for even speaking of this to me," he told Henry, but his voice belied his bravado.

"Fair enough, bear with me for just a minute," Henry signaled Hurricane who just nodded before stepping out of the lounge followed by two of Javier's men who conspicuously did not return.

While they were waiting, Henry summoned a very frightened bartender and ordered a sweet tea for himself and a refresher for the Cuba Libre that Javier was drinking. Not a word was spoken until Hurricane returned with a very ornate woven basket that resembled a yellow acorn with the bright green lid being the cap.

"Thank you, Hurricane," Henry said as he took the basket and set it on a table to Javier's right hand, "Now before I open this present to you, my terms are these. Julius carried a grudge with some of my family. I want these supposed debts canceled immediately, and that is non-negotiable."

There was a brief noise in the room behind them. When Javier looked up, all of his men were on the ground and disarmed. Mike, Jerry, and Hurricane had rendered them unconscious in less than three seconds.

"I should add, Javier, that the reason this basket is sitting here is that Julius tried to harm me and my family, whom I hold very dear to me. You also need to know that I have other baskets," Henry said in a cold tone as he lifted the acorn cap lid from the ornate work.

Javier looked into the open basket at the dead eyes of Julius Salinas staring back at him, and recoiled as if struck by a snake!

"Well, do we have a deal, or do I send for another basket?" Henry asked.

"We have a deal, but tell me your name," Javier didn't take his eyes off the basket.

"Henry Albright," he replied.

"Henry, it is a pleasure doing business with you. Let me buy you and your men a round of drinks to celebrate my promotion," he waved to the bartender, and then to his woman that had been sulking at the end of the bar.

"You should know something about us, Javier. I think that you are the lowest type of vermin on this planet, and I never have dealings with people like you except to put them in the ground. My men are of like mind, and as you have seen, once we are crossed, there is no protection that you can call on that will keep your head out of my basket. Do you understand?" Henry growled at him.

"You will never have to worry about me or my organization again, Señor Albright," Javier struggled to keep the fear out of his voice.

Henry nodded and summoned the men who followed him out without turning their backs on the room. Once in the waiting limo, Henry relaxed.

"Hurricane, have the driver get us to the airport as quickly as possible. One of you call Dixie and tell her to have her plane warmed up and cleared for immediate departure. I've got to call my niece," Henry ordered.

Hanna answered the phone on the first ring, "Hello Uncle Henry. Michael said you were all right, and that we'd be hearing from you. Are you coming to Miami?"

"No Hanna, I'm not. I want you and Tuck to bring the children to Myrtle Beach. It is time to reunite with the family," he told her.

"Uncle Henry, is it over? Is it really over?" She asked, her voice breaking into sobs.

"Yes, Hanna, it is finally over, and it is time for you and Tuck to settle down...at least until the kids are grown," Henry told her, "Now, get everybody ready to travel, and that includes Bob and Abigail. I've got a surprise for you in Myrtle. We'll talk then."

"I love you, Uncle Henry! We'll see you in Myrtle Beach. Just one problem, though, how do I tell Kathryn that I'm not dead?" she asked.

"Gently, Dear, gently," and ended the call.

CHAPTER TWENTY-SIX

Shaun O'Brien fidgeted in the hospital room where he was confined by his weakened heart muscles. The last thing that he ever thought would happen was not being able to take more than a few steps without getting light headed and weak. Now, with no one to talk to except a nurse at the beginning and end of their shifts, he was getting a severe case of cabin fever. Dixie was on his mind also. How could he expect a beautiful creature like her to stick with a crippled up old has been that apparently was now out of a job...if Henry could be believed? Of course, his mind in the quiet intellectual vacuum of the hospital ward rationalized every detail of his supposed problems completely out of proportion to what the reality of the situation was, and Shaun just stewed over them every waking moment.

Late on the afternoon of the sixth day of his hospitalization, a gentle knock sounded at the door.

"Yeah, come on in!" he called.

Dixie Renfroe walked through the door with a big smile on her face, "Hey Shaun, I thought an unannounced visit might be a surprise."

"Dixie! This is a real treat. Get over here and give me a hug!" he replied.

"I'll do better than that!" she exclaimed as she gave him a warm kiss.

"Wow! You do know that the bullet nicked my heart, right?" Shaun kidded as he came up for air.

"You are being silly. I've got some good news for you. They are going to release you into my care in the morning if your tests are okay. If that is all right with you, of course," she said with a smile.

"Dixie, are you sure that you want to be saddled with a worn out old man?" he asked.

"What kind of nonsense is that, Shaun O'Brien? Of course, I want to take care of you until you heal. I thought all of this was settled when you rented my plane!" She fired back, "Now no more of that kind of talk. We are flying home tomorrow unless you want to fly somewhere else where everyone is having a homecoming celebration."

"What are you talking about?" Shaun asked.

"Henry is waiting in Myrtle Beach for you and me to get back there if you can make the trip. Everybody else is there or making their way to the beach for a reunion. Do you want to go or stay up here in the cold for a while?" Dixie asked with a smile.

"I think that I would like to see everyone after almost cashing out. Yeah, Myrtle Beach might be nice," he answered with a big smile.

"We have to make a stop back in Nanaimo and pick up Harry. Henry wanted him at the beach, and I have to cancel a couple of charters and get my planes secured, but we'll leave here as soon as the doctor releases you. Now move over and let me lay down beside you. We can watch TV together," She laughed.

Shaun could feel a panic attack coming on and hoped his newly repaired heart didn't blow up, but between the IV tube and being sandwiched in between the wall and Dixie, there wasn't anything that he could do but lie there and watch life as he knew it...come to an end.

The monotonous tone of the TV soon had them dozing, and the next thing that Shaun knew was that a male nurse was standing inside the room.

"Time for me to check your medication, Mister O'Brien," he said pleasantly.

Shaun was a bit groggy and slow to respond, but something didn't seem quite right, "Kitty was in here about two hours ago to check."

"They have upped your dosage, apparently. This won't take a second," he responded.

It was then that Shaun noticed the tattoo on the man's wrist, an Aztec design bracelet with a '14' just showing from the lab coat sleeve.

"I think we'll pass on the drugs right now. You need to go get your supervisor," Shaun told him quietly but forcefully as his right thumb eased the hammer back on the 1911 behind his right butt cheek.

Dixie was awake now and started to get out of bed, but the man pushed her back down against Shaun while he started to stick the needle into Shaun's IV tube. The next thing that he was looking at was the business end of the 1911 when it came out from under the covers.

"No need for that, O'Brien, I'll just leave," he said with a smile.

"You'll get down on the floor and put your hands behind your head, or you'll fall on the floor!" Shaun barked, "Do it now or die!"

"Okay, okay, I'm doing it," the man dropped to his knees and then face down with his hands behind his head.

"Dixie, go get one of the Mounties. Do it now!" Shaun ordered.

She ran from the room and almost fell over the two men that were on the floor. Dixie looked at them in horror and called back, "He killed the guards, Shaun!"

She heard the .45 ACP fire once just as she made it to the nurse's station where Kitty was slouched forward with her head on the desktop at a funny angle to her body. Trying to keep from screaming, Dixie picked up the phone and dialed the hospital switchboard. It rang three times before an operator picked up.

"This is the ICU floor, the Mounties have been overpowered, and one of the nurses is dead. Please call the police immediately...room 206!" She shouted into the phone.

Dixie ran recklessly back to the room, pausing only long enough to pick up one of the Mounties' pistols. She pushed the door open slowly until she could see the bogus nurse stretched out on his back with a large hole between his eyes, and Shaun sitting on the edge of the bed.

"It's all right now, Dixie. Help me get this IV out and get my clothes on. We're leaving!" Shaun told her, "By the way, toss that piece down over by this jerk before the cops get here. I didn't wait for him to show one when he tried to stand up after you told me what he'd done."

She dropped the pistol and hugged him, "He killed Kitty, Shaun. I thought this was over."

"Well, I don't think that he was one of the ones that Salinas sicced on us. I killed one down in Juarez a few years ago that was sporting that same tattoo. This may have just been a revenge attack," he replied, "Now see if you can find my clothes if you would be so kind."

The door slammed open just then, and the cop that had been Tasered by Tuck and Jerry burst into the room, weapon drawn.

"He's dead, officer. I believe he was Mexican Mafia from the tattoo that I could see," Shaun told him.

"I'm going to have to arrest you for having an illegal firearm in this hospital sir! Stand here and put your hands behind your back!" he ordered.

"You are kidding, right?" Shaun asked.

"If you do not comply, I will use deadly force to subdue you, sir! Hands behind your back!" the cop replied.

While this was going on, two Mounties that had been on watch on the ground floor came into the room. "Officer, you need to stand down immediately! This man is under our protection!"

"He just shot that man, and he might be the one that killed the others out there," the cop shouted back, but he didn't lower his weapon.

During the shouting in the room, Dixie had been forgotten, and she had eased back outside and taken a TASER from the belt of one of the dead guards. Coming back into the room behind the Mounties and the cop who were all facing Shaun, she launched the barbs into the back of the cop who fell twitching and gasping to the floor.

One of the Mounties turned to her, "You'd better let me hold that Ma'am. It will look better on the paperwork."

"Thank you, Sir," she replied quietly as she handed the TASER over and went to Shaun.

"Men, I think it would be best if you could get me somewhere a little safer considering the amount of activity in the past two days here," Shaun said weakly.

"Can you travel, Sir?" The first one asked

"I think so, but I need to get dressed," Shaun replied.

Now the sound of running footsteps filled the hallway outside as teams from the local police and several more Mounties under the jurisdiction of Quincy Stuart arrived.

Shaun dressed as quickly as he could while the Mountie not holding the TASER guarded the door, and then he and Dixie gave them the nod. Just before they made it to the door, the cop on the floor started shouting again and was interrupted by a loud 'BZZZT' as the TASER balled him up again.

"He was starting to be a nuisance," the Mountie shrugged as he jerked the wires clear and walked out of the room leaving the twitching cop on the floor.

"We'll have to get a statement, Mister O'Brien," they told him once they were clear of the room.

"Sure thing men. I have no idea who that guy was. I dozed off, and then he was in the room trying to stick a needle in my IV line. When Dixie screamed at me from outside, he pulled a pistol on me. That's when I shot him in the face with the .45 that one of our men left with me after the last attack," Shaun told them.

Constable Quincy Stuart came up as he finished talking, "Shaun, are you all right?"

"Hi Quincy, I'm sorry about your men, but we are fine," he replied.

"Can you travel? I can get additional information from you by phone, if necessary. I think it might be expedient for you to get somewhere safe right now," Quincy told him in front of the other Mounties.

About then, the cop that they had tased came staggering from the room with his gun in his hand, "You can't release them. That man is my prisoner, and those Mounties tased me."

One of the local police tried to get between him and Shaun but was pushed aside. Almost as if on command, two more Mounties drew TASERs and fired simultaneously, sending him slobbering and twitching in pain to the floor while they disarmed and cuffed him.

"That poor man must have a brain injury or something. How many times did you tase him, Murphy?" Quincy asked his man.

"Oh, a couple I suppose, Inspector. He was a bit rowdy and causing quite a scene," he replied.

Quincy stifled a laugh, "Okay then, release Mister O'Brien and Miss Renfroe so they can get out of here, I'll vouch for them. Shaun, give me a call when you get where you're going, and we'll talk. I'm afraid the drink will have to wait again."

"Thanks, Quincy, I owe you. By the way, little Shaun looks just like you," he replied as he shook Quincy's hand.

"I'll admit to being worried for a few months, Shaun, but he came around," Quincy said with a laugh, "One of these men will give you a lift to the airport, Dixie. Take care of our boy."

"Thank you, Quincy. Please come see us when you can," Dixie shook his hand and turned to go. When they had covered enough distance, she said, "I saw that picture, and that boy looks just like you!"

"I know, and I think Quincy knows also, but that was some years ago, and he married her," Shaun replied.

"Shaun, I'm so nervous and shaky about what happened back there that I don't think I can fly," she told him in the car, "I've never seen that kind of violence before."

"I'll fly us out of here, Dixie. We'll get the dog and head out for Myrtle Beach in the morning. A good night's sleep will do us good," he replied, "I can't believe that you took Henry to Mexico and didn't see some violence."

"No, we went shopping for some new outfits, and I waited with the plane while they did their business. Is Henry a violent man?" she asked.

"Henry is Henry. He is good to those that are loyal, and the Black Plague to those that aren't. He has compassion on old dogs and reserves none for most people, but I wouldn't say that he is violent. Henry Albright can kill calmly when the situation demands it," he told her, "but primarily, he is a businessman and a good man to work for."

CHAPTER TWENTY-SEVEN

Three days after Henry gave them the 'all-clear' report, Tuck and Hanna were ready to fly to Myrtle Beach and the long anticipated reunion with Hanna's step-mother and sisters. The problem was dealing with all of the agencies involved in bringing people back from the dead! After hours of discussions, and one dead end after another, Tuck was so exasperated that he had one of Shaun's reliable sources come up with a package for the family that included passports, drivers' licenses, shot cards, the children's immunization records, and their old social security numbers.

Finally, they boarded a Southwest jet and flew to Myrtle Beach along with Bob and Abigail. Amos and Maggie left the day before to meet Henry and find a condo for each family while the winter rates applied.

"Hanna, I think that Abigail and I should be the ones to break the news to Kathryn and your sisters. They know us, and the shock of seeing you and Tuck right out of the blue might cause a stroke or something," Bob told her on the way to the airport.

"That is a great idea, Bob. I've been worrying what to say or how to say it, but I think we should get into a condo first," she replied.

"Well, it won't take long once that jet takes off, Hanna. If you need to talk, I'll be right there for you," Abigail told her, "Why don't you let me help with the children. Emily can sit with me on the flight."

Tuck was quiet during their conversation so Bob asked him what was on his mind, "You're a little quiet, Tuck. I thought you'd be more excited to get back to being Michael Tucker."

"I'm just thinking about what I can do up here to support the family, Bob," Tuck replied, "There is going to be a real learning curve unless the job entails hunting, fishing, or tracking bad guys."

"I'm sure the Lord has something for you to do, Tuck. We just need to pray about it," Bob tried to reassure him.

"I haven't prayed in so long that I think I've forgotten how. When Harry died, it kind of all went out of me," he replied.

"I only takes the first one to get back to where you were, my friend. God isn't like dealing with the government," Bob laughed.

Tuck gave him a little smile before going back to his thoughts. A few hours later, the Southwest flight touched down in Myrtle Beach, and a very nervous Hanna Tucker, holding the infant Michael Junior, made her way to the baggage claim area behind Abigail and Emily with Bob and Tuck leading the way. She was amazed to see Uncle Henry's big form waiting for them with a beaming smile, and a small crowd gathering around Maggie, who was something of a celebrity in the community. Amos was with the men gathering the small amount of bags that they had brought with them, and the aluminum case that housed Tuck's custom Remington 700 that was like his 'American Express' card.

She gave Henry a big teary hug, "Is it really over, Uncle Henry. I mean REALLY over?"

"Hanna, there is no one looking for you now. I promise," Henry told her as he pulled a Portuguese linen handkerchief from his pocket and dried her eyes, "Have you said anything to Kathryn yet?"

"Bob is going to call her after we get settle," Hanna replied, "We don't want to shock her into a stroke."

"That is a good idea, Hanna. After all of the homecoming celebration, I am going to need to borrow Tuck for a couple of hours this evening, if you don't mind," Henry asked.

"As long as he is not working in the business again, I'm fine with you two talking," Hanna told him.

"No, Tuck is officially retired from Trade Winds Antiques, my dear. This is family business. Now, I've got a limo waiting to take you to the condo, so go tell those boys to get a move on," Henry laughed and left the baggage claim area.

The limo ride to the Sea Watch Condos, where each couple had a two bedroom ocean view condo waiting, was a relatively quiet, short, thirty minute trip from the airport. Hanna nervously played with Emily and the baby as the time for her to see her step-mother and sisters drew near. Finally, they were in the rooms and she had a chance to talk to Tuck before they met up with Bob and Abigail again.

"Michael, does it ever bother you when you kill someone?" she asked him.

"I've not killed anyone that wasn't extremely bad, Hanna, so the answer would have to be 'no'," he replied with a puzzled look on his face, "Why?"

"Because I am almost thirty, and I've killed four people. For Pete's sake, Michael, our little girl is three, and she has seen me kill a man! Not only that, but we've taught her to lie so well, that I can't tell when she is telling the truth anymore. Don't you see the wrong in this?" She ranted with tears in her eyes, "Now I'm going to see Kathryn again, and my sisters, who we told the worst lie to and hurt deeply. Tell me how I am supposed to make this all right."

"I don't have the answer to that, Hanna. We did what we had to do to survive in some pretty tight spots. In spite of everything, we have each other and two beautiful children. Had it not been for your actions, none of this would be happening because we all would be dead, so stop being so hard on yourself," Tuck hugged her as he talked.

"I just keep thinking that we have grown so far away from God, and I feel so empty for it," she told him sobbing.

"I never had the relationship with Him that you did, but I'm kind of feeling the same way. When your Dad was alive, things were sure different," he said, "Maybe we can settle down and find us a church or someplace that we can fit in."

"Do you mean that Michael?" She asked hopefully.

"Of course, I mean it! Now let's go meet Bob and Abigail so the whole family can be together again." he told her.

The plan was that Bob and Abigail would meet Henry at Kathryn's house across the street from the church that Harry Albright had pastored. Once they had broached the subject of Tuck and Hanna being alive along with the children, Bob would call them so that they could reunite.

Tuck and Emily wanted ice cream, so they decided to wait for the call at Friendly's, although Hanna was so nervous that she couldn't eat. Emily was having a good time making a mess of her chocolate and vanilla dish with sprinkles when Tuck's phone finally rang.

"Tuck here," he answered cautiously.

"Tuck, it's Bob. Kathryn passed out when we told her the news, and they've taken her to Grand Strand Hospital," he told him,

"Break that easy to Hanna and come on up. Henry thinks it will be okay."

"How did her sisters react?" Tuck asked with Hanna hanging on every word.

"They're all right. Lots of tears, though, which we expected. You'd better bring a couple of boxes of tissues with you," he replied.

"Did you hear some of that, Love?" Tuck asked Hanna who nodded in the affirmative.

"Tuck, I'm getting off here now. Get your butt to the hospital emergency room!" Bob ended the call.

"Okay Hanna, if you will take Miss Messy to the bathroom and wipe the goo off, I'll take my son. Are you up for this?" he asked.

"Oh Tuck, what if we killed her?" Hanna was aghast.

"Relax, people faint all of the time. Everything is going to be fine, and the reason I know is that your Dad used to tell me that when God made a plan, it always worked out. I believe that Kathryn seeing her grandchildren is one of those plans," he told her.

When they arrived at the hospital emergency entrance, Henry met them in the waiting area.

"Here's the deal, Hanna," he started, "Kathryn is in one of the triage cubicles while they run a few tests. Apparently, she has some heart problems in the past two years that I wasn't made aware of, but she is not in danger."

"What am I supposed to do now, Uncle Henry?" She asked as she started to cry again.

"Your sisters are coming out here in a couple of minutes, and I think the doctor will probably give Kathryn a mild sedative before you see her," he answered, "I'm going back in and send Bob and Abigail out here with the girls."

"I knew that this was a bad idea, Michael. I just knew something like this would happen!" She turned to Tuck who had his hands full with Emily.

"Everything is going to be all right, here come your sisters!" He exclaimed.

Soon the waiting area was filled with the sounds of women crying and hugging. Even the security on duty had eyes full of tears as the story unfolded. Emily was passed around as was Michael Junior, and the tears of joy changed to smiles and laughter within a few minutes. Finally, Henry came out and gathered them together, "Okay, the doctor said that if you are quiet, we can all go back in. Kathryn's been sedated so she shouldn't faint again."

Dixie flew the Beechcraft King Air in to Myrtle Beach from their last stop in Nashville, Tennessee for refueling while Shaun dozed beside her.

"We're almost there, Shaun," Dixie woke him up.

"Okay, I'd better call Maggie and get us a ride. She and Amos are going to share her four-bedroom condo with us, so there will be plenty of room," he told her as he dialed Maggie.

When she got the clearance to land, Dixie made her final approach from the ocean as hundreds of A-10 Warthogs had done in the years that the airport was the Myrtle Beach Air Force Base. When she sat the King Air down, they taxied to a private hangar that Henry had made the arrangements on so that the plane could be serviced while they stayed in Myrtle Beach.

It took thirty minutes before Maggie showed up in a rental to pick them up. She gave Shaun a big hug and then welcomed Dixie in the same way.

"Did Dad give you any trouble, Dixie," she teased.

"Not a bit until I took the duct tape off him," she laughed.

"Very funny, ladies. Where is my son-in-law?" Shaun changed the subject.

"He's with Henry and Tuck on something hush-hush. You know how Henry works," she answered, "Let's get to the condo so you can freshen up."

Dixie wouldn't let Shaun carry the luggage which consisted of her new wardrobe in two suitcases, a large hang-up bag, and a small overnight bag for Shaun.

"I can help with that, you know," Shaun sounded peeved.

"I know, Dear, but the doctor said that there was to be no lifting for at least thirty days. Remember?" Dixie reminded him.

"Dad, we're not going to let you lift a finger while you are recuperating. You might as well get that through that thick skull right now," Maggie told him with a grin, "Also, this condo is one that I bought last year, so you can stay here as long as is needed to heal up before you go traipsing off on any more adventures."

"I'm afraid I'm about adventured out, Maggie, Henry retired me," Shaun suddenly felt older than his sixty-five years.

"If I know you, you won't stay retired very long, but I hope long enough to heal up completely," she replied.

"I'll keep him busy, Maggie," Dixie said, "I'm selling Eagle Air so that I can take care of your dad for a while. That is until he gets tired of me."

Shaun's phone buzzed.

"Excuse me ladies, Henry is on the line," Shaun said with a bit of relief in his voice. The trapped coyote feel had started to come back.

"Henry! What is going on?" he asked.

"Hello, Shaun, did you have a good trip over? Quincy told me what happened at the hospital. I've made contact with Javier, and he assures me that it was not one of his. As a matter of fact, he has his guys out looking for whoever sent your man up there to kill you. How about that?" Henry was ecstatic.

"That's good news, Henry. We had a good flight down here, and the Beechcraft is in the hanger being serviced. We're on the way to Maggie's place for a little R&R." Shaun told him.

"I've got Tuck and your son-in-law with me on a little project. How about if I come by and see you this evening, maybe go out for a bite?" Henry asked.

"Sounds good, Henry. I'll see if my warden will let me escape for a while," Shaun laughed.

"We'll take Dixie with us. This might interest her also. See you tonight," Henry ended the call.

"What did the boss want, Shaun?" Dixie asked.

"He wants to go to dinner tonight," he replied.

"Henry strikes me as the type that never just wants to go to dinner, Dad. He has something up his sleeve," Maggie joined in.

"Henry has always taken care of me where the business has been concerned. I don't have any qualms about discussing some future enterprise with him," Shaun sounded irritated.

"Let's just wait and see what he has to say then. Did he tell you what he is up to with my husband?" Maggie asked.

"No, but I know that he doesn't want them directly involved in the business anymore, so it should be something safe that will keep him home nights," Shaun told her.

"I hope so, Amos and I would like to have a baby," she told them.

"A grandchild for me? I had lost all hope, Maggie. What will he call me?" Shaun asked.

"Why Grandpa of course, silly," she replied, "or Paw Paw, Grandfather, Granddad, or something she makes up. It might not be a boy, you know."

If Shaun heard that, he didn't show it, "A grandson, what do you know? I'm going to be a grandpa!"

CHAPTER TWENTY-EIGHT

"Well, what do you think?" Henry asked Tuck as they pulled into the drive of an old but well-maintained house.

"It sure looks better than most of the new ones with the high pitched steel roof," Tuck answered.

"Five acres of land go with it, and it backs up to the Weyerhauser property," Henry told him, "What do you think?"

"What do I think about what, Henry? It's a nice place," Tuck answered a little puzzled.

"It's miles from the main road, and close to some of the best hunting and fishing around. Now, what do you think?" Henry pressed.

Amos laughed out loud and then thought that he'd better take a little walk around the building where he ran into two men in a South Carolina Department of Natural Resources truck, one of whom was wearing a bit more brass than the other. They waved and then held up their fingers to their lips to signal him to be quiet about their presence. Back in the front of the house, Henry just let Tuck think about his question for a bit, "You know, Tuck, you are a bit slow to be married to my niece. I'm trying to see if you would like to live here and raise the kids here!"

"I don't think that we could afford this, Henry, but yeah, it would be a great place," Tuck replied, the wheels in his head already turning.

Well, this place belongs to me. I bought it last year after an old friend died, and they needed to settle the estate. I am prepared to give you a lifetime lease on it if you want to live here," Henry told him.

"How much would the rent be?" Tuck asked, "and what if I died early. What would happen to Hanna and the kids?"

"How about a dollar per year, with the lease running until the passing of the last member of your immediate family. How does that sound?" Henry laughed.

"It sounds like I don't know how to repay you, Henry. This will make Hanna very happy," Tuck almost choked up.

"Well, there is something else to consider, Tuck. Let's walk around back and see where Amos has gotten off to," Henry said with a meaty arm around Tuck's shoulders.

When they rounded the side of the house and had a full view of the back yard with the parked DNR truck, Tuck stopped and stared for a minute with his mouth agape. There in front of him stood Junior Knowles and Colonel McCreery with Amos in the back grinning from ear to ear.

"Hello, Tuck!" Junior shouted, "Come on over here. The Colonel needs to talk to you."

Tuck hurried over to the two men and shook their hands, "I honestly didn't think that I would ever see you men again."

"Henry told us about the incident down in Texas that forced you folks into witness protection, Tuck. It was certainly a sad day for us at the DNR when we attended your funeral. That being said, I am very interested in your plans now that you are back in the area," McCreery said cheerfully.

"Well, Sir, I really haven't given it much thought. I've been running a charter down in Barbados and helping Henry with an import/export business occasionally. I suppose I will have to find something outdoor related up here to put my hands too," Tuck replied.

"Well, I would like for you to consider coming back to work for us, Tuck. I can pretty much assure you that, given the circumstances behind your resigning, I can have you reinstated to Lieutenant. What do you think?" McCreery asked while Knowles just grinned like his head would split.

"I think that would be wonderful, Colonel, but I really should talk to Hanna about it before I make any decisions. What would be my territory?" Tuck asked.

"Horry County primarily, but you know how it works, you and your men would probably be called out occasionally to help in other areas," McCreery told him, "Let me know by Monday morning, Tuck, and it is good to see you back."

"Yes, Sir, I certainly will," Tuck shook the colonel's hand, "Junior, it's good to see you again also. You've moved up a good bit, haven't you?"

"Just followed that advice you gave me, Lieutenant...that is, Tuck," Knowles gave him a big smile and a handshake, "I hope your wife will let you come back to work with us."

Tuck watched the truck leave the sprawling backyard through a grove of old pecan trees before turning to Henry, "Man, when you throw a surprise party, you don't mess around, do you?"

"So, I take it that you're surprised?" Henry laughed along with Amos.

"I'll say, Uncle Henry, right now I'm hoping that Hanna will let me take my old job back," Tuck replied.

"Well, Amos, have you thought about what you will do now that you're retired?" Henry asked.

"I really haven't given it much thought, Henry. Maggie wants a family so she will probably wean herself from Vanguard. I might take something with one of the airlines out of Myrtle Beach," he replied.

"I've got a friend with U.S. Air that wants to talk to you about flying one of their puddle jumpers. Would you be interested?" Henry asked.

Amos just grinned and shook his hand, "It won't be as butt puckering as flying for you, but, heck yeah, I'd be interested! By the way, Dixie probably is going to opt to stay with Shaun for a while, but Tuck met two pilots down in Jamaica that would really jump at the opportunity to fly for you."

"Is that so? Well, perhaps we can find a way to approach these gentlemen before I need to return home," Henry replied, "In the meantime, maybe you could fly me to Miami to close up the trading company. It won't take more than a few days, and a quick visit would save me a trip back."

"I would be happy to do that, Boss!" Amos exclaimed, suddenly feeling like the mouse that grabbed the cheese before noticing the trap.

"Wonderful, let's get back to Myrtle so we can share the good news with the others, and then get a bite to eat. Deal making always gives me a hearty appetite!" Henry exclaimed.

Dinner that evening was at Rioz in remembrance of Harry Albright, and the last meal that they had eaten out together with him present so many years ago. One of Hanna's sisters kept Emily and Michael Junior, which made the evening that much more relaxing for Hanna and Tuck. Amos and Maggie had been drinking some celebratory wine earlier, and, after many toasts to their plans to have a baby, they were both in their cups. Shaun was more reserved with Dixie, and sat next to Henry so they could discuss a little business over dinner. Bob and Abigail sat next to Hanna and Tuck, and for the most part were quiet about everything that had happened to their friends during the day.

Finally, Bob sensed an opportunity to mention the DNR offer to Tuck, "Are you going to take them up on that offer to reinstate you, Tuck?"

"Well, I do know the job, and we killed that cougar, Bob. The worst that could happen is that I might turn out like you in twenty years or so," he laughed.

Bob smiled at him and waited until the laughter subsided, "Well, that is why I'm asking, Tuck. The DNR changed from the time I went in at about your age until I retired. If you recall, there was quite a bit of political backbiting going on in addition to people trying to kill us. Are you and Hanna up for that?"

"Well, I don't think the politics ever go out of any government agency, but the people killing us thing probably would get a hundred to one from a bookie. Besides, Bob, I'm back home, and Hanna is back home. With the house and a job, we have a real chance for things to return to normal, and that is something," Tuck told him.

"Bob, Tuck is right about this. He came to me to ask what I thought, and I really feel relieved right now," Hanna leaned over to speak, "I've had a rough time since we left here, and that has made it hard on our family. I feel that now the only thing lacking is finding a church family so we can return to some semblance of normalcy."

Bob smiled at Hanna's determination. It was something that had been missing since before they had the opportunity to visit them in

Barbados, and it was a good sign that she was healing from the damage that the stress of the last four years had placed on her.

Abigail chimed in, "Hanna, I want you and Tuck to know that Bob and I will be here for you. We are taking a condo until April or until the Lord decides where we go next."

A voice boomed from further down the table, "BOB, I HEARD YOU BLEW MY CHURCH UP!"

Half the room broke out in gales of laughter.

"It was a leaking gas line, Shaun, and the church is fine. The parsonage will need a little paint, though," Bob replied with a laugh.

At that, the party broke up with everyone in the room still chuckling, but only Henry's table understanding what Shaun was referring to.

Hanna took Tuck aside and whispered, "You need to drive Amos and Maggie back to her condo. They've had too much to drink. I'll go home with Kathryn and pick the kids up. You can come get me there, and we'll spend a little time with her catching up."

Tuck gave her a hug and thanked Henry again, and then hurried to catch Amos.

"Hey Amos, let me drive you guys home," He said.

"It's okay, Tuck, I can make it," Amos replied with a smile.

"No, Dear, Tuck's right. Let him drive while we make out," Maggie told him suggestively.

"Here's the keys, Boy, and step on it!" Amos laughed as he got in the car with Maggie.

Tuck dropped them at Maggie's condo before heading to Kathryn's to pick up Hanna and the children. On the way, his mind rolled over the events of today, and he was amazed that the things that he had just been praying for the day before had all come to pass. They now had a place in the country far enough away from the beach to stay out of the traffic and noise, and he was going to be back with the DNR, something he had specifically prayed for, but thought would never happen in a thousand years. That voice inside his head was back for the first time since they were in Texas, "God works in mysterious ways, Tuck."

"Yes he does, Harry, yes he does."

Shaun and Dixie had waited behind at Henry's invitation to discuss the impending closing of Trade Winds Antiques, something that Henry was reluctant to do, but a necessity with Shaun damaged so severely. He had seen the physician's report on his right-hand man and knew that Shaun had not shared it with Dixie. The bullet that had cut into the heart muscle as it key-holed through Shaun's chest from the back had also shattered his clavicle and drove bone fragments into his lung tissue where the doctors were reluctant to go. It would be a matter of time, possibly a few years, but more likely sooner, that one of these would work its way deeper into the lung and severe an artery leading to an agonizing death. They had debated removing the lung entirely, but Shaun's years of breathing compressed air as a diver had damaged both lungs to the point that one could not keep up with the demand.

"Shaun, I'm in a quandary about the property in Barbados, and I need someone to get down there for a couple of months to see if it would be worth a further investment of time and resources to maintain it. Tuck did quite a job building up the clientele, but with that helper down there trying to run the charters, I'm afraid we might have to let that one go also. What do you think?" Henry asked nonchalantly.

"Well, Henry, I propose that Dixie and I get down there and survey the operation for a couple of weeks. Would that give you the answers that you need?" Shaun asked hopefully, "What do you think, Dixie?"

"Barbados? Are you kidding me? That is a lifetime dream of mine!" She exclaimed excitedly, "Of course we should go down there...to help Henry out of course."

"Of course," Henry replied with a smile, thinking, 'Sometimes people were just too easy to manipulate.'

"Well, it's settled then. Amos and I will fly out as soon as the Beechcraft is ready. Dixie, you and Shaun can tag along and pick up the seaplane in Miami. Shaun has a lot of gear down there anyway, and it will give you an opportunity to shop for Island clothes. Tomorrow, Shaun, you and Tuck should get together and discuss the details of the Barbados operation. Have you thought about the ministry in Honduras?" Henry asked.

"Yes, I think that we'll appoint one of the associate pastors into the main pastor's role. It will relieve the stress from Bob and Abigail while they are here, and I really can't pretend to be a pastor any longer," he replied.

"It's settled then! You two will have a working holiday with all expenses paid, while Amos and I work our butts off in Miami," Henry slapped his hand on the table top, startling the people at the next table, "I would like to leave the day after tomorrow if that works for you."

"We are on your clock again, Henry. Of course, it works," Shaun shook Henry's hand.

"Well, I have a date with a dog, see you in the morning," Henry proclaimed jovially as he left the table.

CHAPTER TWENTY-NINE

Mick Donaldson, a young man in his early twenties, watched the odd looking single engine SeaStar seaplane taxi up to the dock, and hoped it would bring him news of George and Stephanie Alexander, who had disappeared a few weeks before, leaving him alone to run the charter boat that he had worked as the first mate on. His face lit up in a grin as he recognized Shaun O'Brien climbing out of the cockpit.

"Mister O'Brien!" He shouted, waving his arms to get Shaun's attention.

"Hey, Mick, how are you?" Shaun shouted back as he helped Dixie climb out of the plane.

Mick came running up to help with the luggage, "I'm fine, Sir, but George and Stephanie left with the kids, and I've not heard a word from them."

"George says to tell you that he is terribly sorry, but they had a family emergency and had to leave on very short notice," Shaun told him, "That's why Dixie and I are down here. We heard that you needed help, and wanted to come down and see if the business was worth saving."

"Well, Mister O'Brien, I've been running the few charters that are on the books, but folks have been canceling when I tell them that George is not here," Mick replied, "By the way, George left the Jeep in the parking lot, and I don't have a key. I've had to haul ice and stuff by hand," he told Shaun.

"I've got the keys right here, Mick. If you can put the luggage in and give us a ride to the house, I'll let you use it to haul whatever supplies you need for the next trip," Shaun tossed him the keys.

"That's a relief because we have a big one tomorrow morning!" Mick exclaimed, "I hate to bring this up, but George used to pay me after the charters were finished, and I haven't been paid for the last five."

"I'll take care of that in the morning, Mick, right now here's a fifty. Will that help?" Shaun handed him the bills.

"Thank you, Sir. I'll be by the house at seven in the morning to pick you up," he replied as he started to leave.

"Well, take us to the house before you run off," Shaun reminded him.

"Yes, Sir, I'm sorry. I'm just a little nervous is all," Mick grabbed the bags and headed for the Jeep followed closely by Shaun and Dixie who exchanged questioning looks with each other.

They made the quick trip to the house that Tuck and Hanna had used and unloaded their bags. Mick roared off in the Jeep as if he had an appointment that he was late to.

"Dixie, I'm getting a feeling that something is not quite right with that boy," he told her.

"Normally, I would say that you're imagining things, Shaun, but I've got the same feeling," she replied, "Are you well known down here?"

"Well, I've been here enough that the locals know me...why?" he told her.

"One of us needs to do some checking, and I think that it is me. I'll just change real quick, and put on my new shades...see, just another tourist," she laughed.

"Okay, but if you see anything wrong, come back and get me. Don't say anything to anybody, understood?" He told her.

"Worrywart! Relax, I'll be fine," and she was out of the door, headed in the direction of the island marina shop where the Jeep was now parked.

Shaun went into the bedroom with the bags and opened his to take out his 1911 and two magazines of ammo. He removed the M-4 and the suppressor and hid it between the mattress and box spring for a just in case moment, should it arise. He then went out on the porch and waited with his cell phone in his hand.

Dixie walked into the marina store and stayed close to the displays of tee shirts and tackle as if she was shopping. From the back of the store, she heard the sound of shouting as a man's voice sounded like it was raised in anger, but she couldn't make out what he was saying. The other voice that was protesting had to be Mick. Dixie needed to get closer without attracting the attention of the tired looking, slightly overweight girl that was playing with her cell phone at the cash register. She moved to a drink refrigerator that was just down from the oblivious girl and acted like she was pondering her selection, but it turned out to be the ideal place to hear the conversation in the back room.

"But Marcy and the baby haven't had anything but peanut butter in a week, Mister Greene, and we have another man down to run the boat. I'll have the money tomorrow...I promise. I just need some food on credit tonight," Mick's voice came to her ears.

"This fifty just barely covers the interest on what I've loaned you, boy. No more credit until I get all of my money. I don't care if your trash wife and kid eat or not!" The man answered roughly.

There was a sound of a scuffle followed by a thud as something heavy hit the floor, and the owner came out of the back rubbing his right hand which he immediately used to slap the pudgy girl on the rump.

Dixie stepped outside and called Shaun, "You need to get over here to the marina store. Mick has had a little trouble with the store owner."

"I'll be right there," and he hung up.

Shaun came through the door of the marina shop just as Mick staggered out of the back room with a badly swollen right eye and a bloody nose. Dixie took the staggering young man by the arm and led him outside to a chair on the porch.

"Why hello, Mister O'Brien." Mister Greene said when he saw Shaun, "It's been a long time."

He stuck out his hand to shake Shaun's and was immediately jerked toward the large man, and then hit squarely in the face by Shaun's large left fist hard enough to break the cartilage in his nose and sit him down squarely with a loud thump.

"You've got something that belongs to my mate, Greene, give it to me," Shaun threatened.

The man reached into his shirt pocket and took the fifty dollars out, "He owes this to me. I've been carrying him and his trash wife for the last two weeks!"

"How much does he owe you without interest?" Shaun asked, still standing over Greene.

"I let them have about a hundred in toiletries and canned goods, but I have a right to charge interest!' he protested.

Shaun reached down and jerked the fifty from the man's hand, "You've been stealing from the locals and tourists for years,

Greene. Mick's account is going to be marked 'paid in full' or you are going to leave the island. Do I make myself clear?"

Greene glared at Shaun for a minute while the stories that he had heard about this man ran through his memory, "I guess, Shaun. I didn't mean anything."

"You'll also apologize to the boy for bad mouthing his wife," Shaun told him as Dixie brought Mick back in.

"Okay, Okay, I'm sorry Mick that I called Marcy trash, and you don't owe me anything," he told him with a red face.

Mick just stood there for a minute staring down at the low life that was sitting on the floor in front of him before delivering a kick to the man's groin area that would have made a Rugby player proud. Greene screamed in pain as the kick lifted his rear off of the floor and then fell over on his back while holding the injured area in both hands. Shaun stared in disbelief, and then followed an equally amazed Dixie outside where Mick had walked to.

"That was unexpected, Mick, but a great shot if I do say so," Shaun handed him the fifty, "Where did you learn to fight dirty, anyway?"

"George showed me, Sir. Listen, I appreciate everything, Mister O'Brien, but I need to get home to Marcy and the baby. I think I'll take them out for a burger tonight," Mick told them and walked off.

"Hey Mick, take this and get her a steak. Winners need to eat real meat!" Shaun handed him another fifty.

"I'll see you at seven. Sir," the boy told them with a big grin.

"Shaun, what is going to happen to that family if we close down the charter business?" Dixie asked.

"I must be getting soft in my old age, Dix, but I think we can get Henry to work a deal with that young fellow to take this over in time. First, we need a few weeks of R&R!" He replied as she squeezed his hand.

The safe house complex in Miami was quiet with all of the men on a well-deserved vacation following Henry's rescue, so Henry and Amos decided to stay there instead of paying for a hotel room. The first day after their arrival, Amos was acting as a traffic cop as numerous attorneys were brought in to secure the business that had been known as Trade Winds Antiques, Inc., but was really a cover for the host of clandestine operations that had spanned the globe for the past twenty years. Now, without his right-hand man, and the wake-up call that the kidnapping had given him, Henry Albright was ready to quietly fade out of the professional vigilante business, and resume his quiet life in Washington State.

After two days of papers being signed, the business and its subsidiaries had been closed down with the exception of the small charter operation in Barbados, which Henry had quietly signed over to Shaun O'Brien. He knew that Shaun had the capital to keep the business running, and wanted his faithful friend to have a decent finish to what had been a rough life. With everything in place, Henry decided to return to Myrtle Beach for a few days before heading back to Washington, but there was a problem of being short a pilot unless Amos could renew his contact with Reginald's men in Kingston.

"Amos, I need for you to try and get the contact information of those pilots that work for Reginald Smythe," Henry told him over dinner, "If they are interested, have them meet us here, and we'll fly them back to Myrtle with us."

"I'll see what I can do, Boss," Amos answered, "Tuck gave me a piece of paper with their names on it before we left."

After dinner, Amos started calling the numbers that he had for the men, and, after several attempts, the younger of the two answered his call.

"This is Edmund Carver speaking. How may I help you?" He asked.

"Edmund, this is Amos Whitehorse. I was the pilot that you shanghaied to Honduras a few weeks back. Do you remember me?" Amos asked.

"How could I forget, Sir?" He replied in a confused tone.

"Edmund, you mentioned to my traveling companion that you wanted a new job. Were you serious about that?" Amos asked.

"Very much so, Sir. Reggie fired us after he got out of the hospital, and there is not much here in the way of work," came the reply.

"How soon can you be in Miami, Edmund? I have a job for you and your buddy if he is interested," Amos told him.

"Arthur met with an unfortunate accident right after we were terminated, Sir. Had I been the senior on the flight, I probably would have been killed also. As it is, I'm just getting back to where I can tie my shoes without passing out," Edmund replied, "but I can be in Miami tomorrow evening, and I can pass a flight medical."

"There will be a ticket waiting for you at the airport counter in about an hour. I'll pick you up in Miami. One other thing,

Edmund, do not tell anyone where you are going. Is that understood?" Amos cautioned.

"Perfectly, Sir. I will see you tomorrow evening, and thank you for the opportunity!" Edmund ended the call.

Amos spent the next hour booking the flight for Henry's new pilot and then decided to wait on the maintenance check on the Beechcraft until the next day since they had to be at the airport anyway. It was a decision that he would live long enough to regret.

It was already late afternoon before Edmund's flight touched down, and well into twilight by the time that he appeared at the luggage carousel. Amos spotted him after sweeping the room and took Henry over to meet his new pilot.

"Boss, meet Edmund Carver, the pilot that we've told you about. Edmund, this is your new employer, Henry Albright," Amos introduced them.

"Please to meet you, Sir. Thank you for hiring me sight unseen," Edmund spoke nervously.

"Relax, Edmund. You'll find that this job will be more relaxing than your last. Now, we are in a rush, so let's grab your bag and get to our plane, shall we?" Henry told him.

They made the trip from the airport to the private hanger where the Beechcraft had been rolled out onto the apron and were met by a coverall wearing mechanic.

"She's fueled and ready, Sir," he said to Amos, "I also did a routine maintenance check and everything is ship shape.

Amos was uneasy about having someone else do his maintenance checks, but they were running late, and he didn't like flying over the ocean in the dark.

"How much is the tab?" Henry asked.

"The company will bill you, Sir. Have a nice flight," the mechanic walked back inside the hanger.

"You heard the man, the ship is ready and so am I!" Henry declared, "Let's get back to Myrtle Beach!"

"Okay, Edmund, you take the co-pilot chair and we'll get this bird in the air," Amos told the new pilot as they boarded. He closed the door and secured it after Henry was seated.

Amos quickly ran through the pre-flight check with Edmund, and then the two big turboprops roared to life.

"This is Beechcraft Mike, Alpha, Golf, Alpha One Niner Seven to tower requesting clearance, over," Amos radioed.

"Beechcraft Mike, Alpha, Golf, Alpha One Niner Seven, you are clear on runway seven. Have a good flight, over," the radio crackled.

"Up, up and away!" Amos called as he shoved the throttles up and proceeded with his signature fighter style takeoff.

Soon they were cruising at twenty thousand feet and skirting the coastline, but by the time they reached Northern Florida, they would be a hundred miles off the coast and over a rougher Atlantic Ocean, something that always made Amos slightly uncomfortable at night.

Henry had laid his seat back for comfort while he took a nap, and his snoring was audible in the cockpit. Amos decided to find out what he could about Edmund.

"Edmund, I thought that you told us that you were married when my colleague started to throw you out of that Cessna," Amos said.

Edmund hesitated a minute, and a bead of sweat became visible in the low light on his forehead, "I am married, Sir, and I have a five-year-old son."

"Why are you so nervous? Are you afraid that the job won't work out?" Amos asked, now a trifle suspicious.

"No, Amos. I would like very much for the job to work out so that I can bring my family to the States and get them away from Mister Smythe," he replied, but now there were tears in his eyes.

Alarms started going off in Amos' mind at the mention of Reginald's name, "What have you done, Edmund? Did you tell Reggie that you were coming to see me?"

"Please, Amos, he has my wife and said he would kill her if I didn't tell him where I was going. That's why I told him," he answered.

"HENRY! WAKE UP, WE HAVE A PROBLEM!" Amos yelled to the sleeping man in the back of the plane.

Henry made his way toward the cockpit and leaned in, "What's the problem, Amos?"

"This dipstick told Reggie where he was going, and who he was going with," Amos told him, "and I didn't do my own maintenance check on this aircraft before we left! That's the problem!"

"Edmund, what did your old boss plan to do to this plane?" Henry leaned toward him in a threatening gesture.

"I don't know, Sir. He slapped my wife in the face, and told me to go ahead with my plans," Edmund told him, trembling with fear.

"What kind of a weak-kneed suck up would leave his wife with a man like that? I think that I will do her a favor and kill you myself!" Henry's temper was boiling, "Where are we, Amos?"

"We are about seventy miles off of Brunswick, Georgia, Boss. I'm going to change direction and try to find a place to set down. If I know Reggie, and I do, he has had someone rig this plane to disappear!"

"I'll see if there is anything out of the ordinary in the cabin," Henry told him, and started a thorough search of the cabin area...to no avail, "She's clean back here, Amos. I'm thinking that there is a bomb in the baggage compartment with a GPS trigger on it, or maybe barometric."

Amos had made the turn toward a small airfield in Brunswick when both the port and starboard engines belched flames and smoke simultaneously.

"GPS, Henry! I just lost both engines. You had better buckle up!" Amos shouted, "Edmund, I'm going to kill you later, but right now, I need for you to feather both props while I try to glide this thing closer to land."

Amos grabbed the headset, "Mayday, Mayday, Mayday, any station. This is Beechcraft Mike, Alpha, Golf, Alpha One Niner Seven. We have engine failure and are going to ditch off of Brunswick, Georgia. Mayday, Mayday, Mayday, please respond, over."

"Beechcraft Mike, Alpha, Golf, Alpha One Niner Seven, this is the trawler Sea Wolf, Alpha Whiskey Foxtrot, One Seven Six Fiver. We can give support until someone else arrives. What is your location, over?"

"Sea Wolf, Alpha Whiskey Foxtrot, One Seven Six Fiver, we are heading due west at one hundred and seventy knots and descending below fifteen thousand feet. I've just passed North 31 degrees, 1 minute and West 80 degrees and two minutes. Can you relay this information to the Coast Guard and anyone monitoring? I've got my hands full up here, over?" Amos replied.

"Glad to help. We are within ten miles from where you might come in. The ocean is a brisk five to eight feet, which might be a problem, over." the trawler captain responded.

"Ten–four Sea Wolf, please repeat our mayday to Savannah Coast Guard, and give them our location, over."

"Will do, good luck to you, out" the Sea Wolf ended communication, but then the radio was filled with the mayday being repeated by several vessels to the Coast Guard in Savannah.

"Edmund, I need that starboard prop feathered or it is going to tear the engine loose from the wing!" Amos told him as he tried to hold the airspeed above stall and milk a few more miles in the glide.

It won't feather, Amos. I've tried the controls several times," Edmund told him as the vibration from the wildly spinning prop on the damaged starboard engine threatened to take the wing off.

"Henry, we've got a couple of minutes if the wing holds before we hit the drink. Can you get that life raft out of the storage in the back, and then strap back in?" Amos shouted over the noise.

"I'm on it, Boy. You just get us down in one piece or you're fired!" Henry shouted back.

"Right Oh, Chief. I'd hate to tell Maggie that I got fired from a job that I volunteered for!" Amos laughed.

"How can you laugh at a time like this?" Edmund asked, just short of hysterics.

"Because, Edmund, I know where I'll end up if we don't make it, and it is a darn sight better than where I am now. Besides, I'm a

Navy fighter jock. This is nothing compared to landing on a carrier deck in a storm." Amos answered.

Just as he finished, the starboard prop shaft broke just ahead of the engine, and the wildly spinning blades screamed toward the cabin and Edmund.

If he had noticed, there would have been no time to scream, and Amos was suddenly sitting next to the young man that had been violently cut almost in two from his right shoulder to his leg.

"My wife..." was all that came weakly from his mouth as the life's blood spilled from his body in seconds.

Combat experience was all that kept Amos from jumping out of his seat and leaving the cockpit as he stared at the bloody wreck of a man that he had just been talking to, and just as suddenly as the prop had killed Edmund, the vibration was gone, and the plane had become controllable in the glide again.

"Amos, are you all right?" Henry called.

"I'm fine, Henry, but Edmund is cut in half!" Amos told him.

"Get us down, Amos. I'm ready to get out of this thing," Henry replied, the stench of the intestines and blood making him feel sick.

"Yes, Sir, that is going to happen without much input from me in about two minutes," Amos told him, "Hold on!"

With the wind at their tail, Amos decided to try to land with the sea at their back and slightly quartering. He hoped that by doing that, it would stay afloat long enough for them to escape. There was time for one more call,

"Mayday, Mayday, Mayday, this is Beechcraft Mike, Alpha, Golf, Alpha One Niner Seven, we are going in at coordinates North 31 degrees, 1 minute and West 80 degrees and two minutes, out," Amos finished the call and took the headphones off. He then took his wallet out, and reached over to the body next to him and removed Edmund's wallet and ID from his left side coat pocket, replacing it with his.

The plane hit the top of an eight-foot wave and skipped over the next one, slamming nose first into the third before slewing around. The damage from the loose prop caused a massive tear in the cabin on impact with the water, and Amos struggled with Henry to get the door open on the rapidly sinking plane. They finally managed to push it open and get the raft out as the plane started to roll on its port side.

"Jump, Henry! I'm right behind you!" Amos shouted and gave the big man a push.

Once in the water, Henry pulled the cord to inflate the raft, and both men clambered in. They were hoping for a quick rescue, but thankful to be alive.

"Are you okay, Henry?" Amos asked.

"My right ankle is broken, but everything else seems to be working. How about you?" he responded.

"The belt cut me on impact, but nothing is broken. Can you reach that flare gun in the container?" Amos asked.

Henry passed the flare gun up and Amos fired a red flare straight up over the small raft.

"Hopefully the Sea Wolf will see that, Henry. If not, the Coast Guard should be around by morning," Amos told him.

"I'd be all right if this rubber piece of crap would quit bouncing around. My ankle is killing me," Henry growled.

Ten minutes later, the blinding light from a ship's floodlight illuminated the raft and the plane which was still floating with the tail section above water.

"Ahoy there," came a voice from the direction of the light.

"Ahoy, are you the Sea Wolf?" Amos called.

"We are indeed, Sir. Let's get you men aboard," the skipper called.

"Be careful of my friend, his ankle is broken, and our pilot, Amos Whitehorse was killed in flight," Amos replied.

Henry just gave him a questioning look, but Amos shook his head slightly to keep him quiet.

Twenty minutes later, a buoy had been attached to the fuselage of the partially sunken plane as a warning to any ship traffic in the area, and the Seawolf was steaming toward Brunswick for a rendezvous with a cutter out of Savannah.

Henry sat at the galley table and grimaced as one of the fishermen wrapped the badly swollen ankle with an Ace bandage, and the duty cook, another fisherman, poured some hot coffee.

"I'm Captain Gene Collins, but my friends call me 'Steamin' Gene'," the Captain introduced himself.

"I'm Edmund Carver from Jamaica, and this is my employer, Henry Albright, Captain," Amos told him.

Henry followed his lead and said, "I just hired this man to fly for me to replace that Amos Whitehorse. He was a good bit of trouble, and I hope he is in a better place."

Amos scowled, "I hope this doesn't mean that I'm losing this job, Boss. I can drive your car also."

Henry was silent for a minute, "Well, I do need a gardener and someone to walk my dog occasionally. What do you think...Edmund?"

"I think I'll go back to Jamaica, Mon!" Amos replied and both men laughed.

They were interrupted by one of the deckhands, "Captain, the Coast Guard is on the radio. They want to talk to you."

"Excuse me, fellas. I'll go see what they are up to," Captain Gene said as he left the galley.

"You are headed for Jamaica, or I miss my guess. How many men do you need?" Henry leaned over and asked.

"Well, at least Mike and Jerry. Hurricane would be an asset. What about Shaun?" Amos answered.

"Shaun is off the list. That bullet damaged his heart," Henry told him, but didn't elaborate, "Tuck would be my choice to head this operation, but Hanna will kill me if I ask him."

"I need to call Maggie and prep her for the news that I'm dead. I sure don't want her to hear it from the tube!" Amos said, "This needs to happen quickly, and you should know that I intend to kill that snake in a very painful fashion."

"I don't need to know the details, just make sure you drop Edmund's ID somewhere close to the body when it's finished," Henry agreed with the plan.

"Hey, Guys, those Coast Guard people sure must like you. A sea rescue chopper is circling us right now!" Gene shouted from the wheelhouse.

"Well, it looks like the vacation is over," Henry said to no one in particular, "Come on, Edmund, let's get back in the air."

CHAPTER THIRTY

The plan was simple as plans go. Amos would meet Jerry, Mike, and Hurricane in Miami, and then they would take Shaun's crew boat conversion to Jamaica. From a safe harbor, they would make their way to Reggie's office in Kingston, and play the rest by ear. What they had not counted on was Shaun getting the word via a Caribbean news channel and thinking that the father of his future grandson had been killed in the crash. When that news filtered in two days after the incident, Shaun left Dixie in charge of the charter business and flew the SeaStar to Miami. As Amos' luck would have it, Shaun was with Jerry in the garage of the safe house when Amos showed up and had already been briefed on the pending operation.

"There you are! What is the meaning of scaring your father almost to death? I want to know the details, and you'd better make this good, or my daughter will truly be a widow!" Shaun fumed.

"Well, we've got things to get ready, so I'm just going to go with the crew and leave you two alone," Jerry said as he fast-walked to the door.

"Look, Shaun, Henry said that you were still recuperating and didn't want me to tell you about this job. Reginald Smythe sabotaged the plane and blew the engines over the ocean. His man was killed when a prop cut through the cabin, so I swapped IDs with him to throw Reggie off. I'm going back there to kill him, and whatever crew he has working for him," Amos gave him the condensed version.

"Why don't you let me take care of this, and you get home to Maggie?" Shaun asked.

"That worthless pile of dung tried to have us all killed when Tuck brought the family to Miami. That mess in Honduras was him," Amos told him, "Tuck roughed him up pretty badly, but made the mistake of leaving him alive. I'm not about to make that mistake again."

"It will take at least a week to get there in that crew boat, and I've got the SeaStar with me. This operation could be over with tomorrow evening," Shaun replied, "Besides, I can be the lookout, and just chill with the plane."

"I want that Cessna that he has to make up for the Beechcraft, so I can't kill him until he signs the paperwork," Amos explained the plan.

"Amos, killing a man up close is a lot different than shooting one from twenty miles out with a missile, and I don't particularly want my grandson's father to be like me. If you want the plane, I'll put you in the plane, but you need to leave while Reggie is still alive. Do you understand?" Shaun told him forcefully.

"I hadn't thought that far ahead, to be honest, Shaun. There is also Edmund's wife and kid. If they are being held by Reggie, I need to take them with me," he added.

"I will agree to that only if they are immediately in the vicinity, otherwise, you and Hurricane fly back to Miami, and I'll take Jerry and Mike with me to take care of Reggie after you've got a head start," Shaun was adamant.

"Henry is going to be pissed!" Amos sounded worried.

"So? You don't work for Henry. You are married to my daughter, and you'd better not forget that little nugget of truth!" Shaun slapped him on the back, "Come on, the boys will be ready to leave by now."

"Got room for one more?" Tuck asked as he walked through the garage door with his 'toolkit' in his hand.

"Tuck, I thought you were going to take that DNR job in South Carolina!" Amos replied in surprise.

"That is next week. When Henry told us what you were up to, Hanna insisted that I come along and keep you out of trouble," Tuck told him, "Hey, Shaun, fancy meeting you here."

"Tuck, I'm glad to see you. How about a little piracy before you return to being an honest wage earner?" Shaun laughed.

"I'm up for it. To tell you the truth, I have had misgivings about letting Reggie off the hook so easy the last time we met. By the way, Amos, Maggie sent this to you," Tuck said as he handed Amos an envelope.

Amos ripped it open and took out a pregnancy tester that showed a positive result.

"Well, Grandpa, you'd better be sure I get back here in one piece or you'll be babysitting while Maggie goes back to work!" Amos laughed as he handed the tester to Shaun, "You fellows will have to excuse me, I've got to check in with the Boss."

Tuck laughed at the look on Shaun's face and then got serious, "Shaun, Henry told me about the prognosis with your lungs. Are you certain that you want to be on this op?"

"Tuck, this is what I do. I'm not a charter boat skipper anymore than you were. Knowing that Maggie is pregnant sheds a different light on things, but the bottom line for me is making sure that Amos gets home in one piece. Besides, I'm just the planner on this one," Shaun replied, "Go squeeze in with the others, and we'll be along directly."

Tuck left and Shaun went into the small office area of the garage to rummage one of his desk drawers. He stepped back out just as Amos came back in from his phone call.

"Amos, come over here a minute and look this over for me," Shaun called to him and pointed into the office at a chart that was lying on the desk.

"Sure thing, Grandpa," Amos laughed as he stepped inside and leaned over the chart.

Moving quickly, Shaun stuck a needle in Amos' neck and mashed a plunger to inject one of his knockout concoctions into Amos' bloodstream.

"What?" Amos managed to gasp as his hand went to his neck.

"You go back home when you wake up and love on my daughter and grandson," Shaun said as he eased him into the desk chair before walking out and locking the door behind him.

Shaun walked to the SUV holding the waiting team and got in.

"Where's Amos?" Tuck asked.

"Headed home," Shaun replied.

The men just exchanged knowing glances.

"Okay Boss, what's the plan?" Tuck questioned.

"We are going in quietly and bringing Mister Smythe out. I don't want so much as a footprint to let anyone know we were there, if we can help it," Shaun told him so that everyone could hear, "We'll work the details out on the flight, but everything that Amos talked about is void. Smythe is the only one coming out with us. Tuck and Hurricane will handle the extraction while Jerry and Mike cover."

Shaun pulled his cell phone and dialed Henry, "Henry, Shaun here. As we discussed earlier, Amos is in my office in the safe building and should be waking up in about six hours...give or take. Can you have him delivered to Maggie for me?"

"Of course I will. Is the team assembled?" Henry asked.

"We are underway," Shaun replied, "Any special orders?"

"No, just send my nephew back in one piece, if possible," Henry replied and ended the call.

They arrived at the dock thirty minutes later and climbed into the cramped passenger compartment of the small SeaStar after stowing their gear.

"Okay men, here is the basic plan. I'm going to fly across Cuba to the Siguanea Airport on the other side. We can refuel at the Colony Hotel dock where I have a meeting with one of the Cuban authorities concerning a very large bounty on the head of a Reginald Smythe. Keep a low profile there, the less they see, the fewer questions we will have to answer. Now buckle up," Shaun told them as he fired the turboprop and taxied out for takeoff.

An hour later, the refueling was complete, so Tuck and Hurricane pulled the men's bags quickly from the luggage hold and handed them inside. While they waited for Shaun to conclude his business, the men prepped the tools of their trade to be ready for the next stop. Thirty minutes later, they were back in the air and headed for Kingston, Jamaica. While Shaun flew the SeaStar, Tuck went over the map of the targeted area with the men. It was decided that they would make a landing outside of the harbor close to the Caribbean Maritime Institute and taxi in. Reginald Smythe was reported to be using one of the condos close to the harbor as his home when he wasn't in his office that was located in the institute building.

The sea was smooth and the sky dark under the new moon as Shaun expertly brought the plane into a picture perfect landing and taxied into the harbor entrance, where they moored quietly at a fuel dock that was deserted at this hour.

"According to our latest source, Reggie is in number one twenty-seven, down on the other end of the harbor. Take only the dart guns, and try not to use them if you don't have to. Once you have him, we'll drop him back in Cuba," Shaun briefed them.

Tuck had Mike and Jerry work the back of the condo complex until they got in position behind Smythe's unit, and then he knocked on the door which was answered by one of Reggie's guards.

"Hello, sir. I'm looking for Priscilla Alston. Is she home?" Tuck asked.

"There is no one here by that name!" The man replied and tried to shut the door, but Tuck had his foot in the jamb.

"She's a dark haired girl about twenty-five. You must have seen her!" Tuck tried his best to act slightly drunk.

The man reached to push Tuck away from the door when a massive hand grabbed his and pulled him out of the doorway. Hurricane had been out of sight beside the door waiting for that opportunity. Before he could sound an alarm, Tuck stuck him in the neck, and they hid him in the short shrubbery under the window.

They walked slowly into the entryway and stopped when a voice that Tuck recognized as belonging to Reggie called out, "Who was it?"

"It was nuh one, just ah drunk," Hurricane replied in a perfect Patois accent.

"Very good, Henry, would you bring my drink when you come back in?" Reggie replied.

Hurricane shrugged his shoulders at Tuck before answering at Tuck's nod, "Sure, Bass."

Tuck took the dart gun and looked slowly around the corner. Standing in the middle of the living room, Reggie had his back to them and was facing an attractive young woman that looked directly at Tuck.

"Marcy, Edmund will be back here shortly, and then, if you are 'nice' to me, I will let you and the child go with him," Reggie told her.

Tuck realized that the element of surprise might be gone in a second, shot a dart into Reggie's neck just as Mike and Jerry came in through the back door. They heard two soft pops of the dart guns back there, and the two more thuds as bodies hit the floor.

Marcy just stood, frozen in fear as Hurricane took aim with his dart.

"Don't shoot her, she's not going to tell anyone that we were here, are you?" Tuck spoke to both.

"No, I just want to go home with my baby," she replied in perfect English.

"Are you Marcy?" Tuck asked.

"Yes, why?" she replied.

"I've got some bad news for you Marcy. Edmund is dead, and I'm sorry that we don't have time to sugar coat it, but you need to get as far away from here as possible tonight," Tuck told her.

"I thought that he might be, I overheard Reggie talking to his men about an accident," she replied in tears, "We'll be all right."

"Well, let's get this one out of here," Tuck grabbed a corner of Reggie, and the others each got a hold on him, "You've got about thirty minutes before these others wake up Marcy."

"It will be enough time," she replied as she headed off to get her son, but not before making a stop in Reginald's office where the safe was standing open.

"Took you long enough!" Shaun exclaimed as they threw their captive on the floor of the SeaStar, and then stepped on him multiple times as they loaded in themselves after Tuck cast off the mooring line.

Shaun didn't try to hide as they started to taxi out to open water. He pushed the throttle up to unleash the full seven hundred and twenty horsepower of the turboprop, and the loaded plane was airborne when the first gentle wave raised her bow.

"Next stop Cuba! Was there any trouble?" Shaun asked.

"Well, we left a young lady pilfering old Reggie's safe, and three guards with headaches, but other than that, it was a routine op," Tuck laughed with the others.

Shaun called his contact in Cuba, "Hello Ramon, I've got your merchandise. Have you got the authorization on the reward yet?"

"Shaun O'Brien, have I ever failed you on a business deal?" the general replied, "It will be in your bank account before you get here."

"Very good, my friend. I'll be dropping the package at the dock in about an hour," Shaun ended the call.

"Tuck, check that account for the deposit. I have a feeling that we are being hoodooed by my good friend, Ramon," Shaun told him.

Tuck spent the next few minutes accessing the Cayman Islands account that they sometimes used for small job payments, especially those that might skirt certain legalities a bit.

"Nothing yet, Shaun. Do you think they will pay?" Tuck asked.

"I think that they will try to waylay us if we show up at the Colony Hotel. It will cost about, oh say, one hundred thousand dollars to ransom ourselves and the plane...if they let us keep the plane," Shaun replied, "I anticipated this, so on to plan 'B'."

Shaun called General Ramon again, "Ramon, there has been a problem with the wire transfer. I really need to see that money in my account before Mister Smythe can be dropped off. It's just business, you understand."

"Yes, Shaun, I understand completely. One of my incompetent aides was supposed to process that for me, but he screwed it up, as usual. Now, when it is in your account, you will drop our package at the Colony Hotel pier, right?" Ramon asked.

"I'm on the way now, General. You probably should polish your dress shoes for the medal ceremony when you turn this one in," Shaun joked with him.

"Check it now, my friend. It should be in there," Ramon assured him.

Tuck checked, "It just came through, exactly one hundred thousand."

"We've got it, Ramon. The package is on the way," Shaun ended the call, "Get ready to put down, boys. Reggie is going to get out at the Castillo de Morro in Ciudamar in about fifteen minutes."

"Boy is old Ramon going to be pissed at you!" Tuck laughed with the men.

"That old goat enjoys the chase. Besides, in the end he gets what he wants, just not bragging rights to how he got one over on Shaun O'Brien," Shaun laughed with them.

Shaun made a low pass over the inlet that was guarded by the famous fort, and they saw that it was empty of any vessel lights. He came in for a landing close to the beach opposite the old Castillo, and the team made quick work of getting Reggie, who was now trussed like a pig in layers of quick ties and Gorilla tape, to the beach, just above the tidal mark before returning to the plane. Shaun got it back in the air quickly and headed for points East just off the deck to keep the composite-bodied plane off the radar until they were away from Cuba airspace. The Naval Air Station at Gitmo was an option if they were discovered, but it would be hard to get the plane out of there without having a mad Cuban general put a missile up the pipe.

They finally got out of Cuban airspace without an incident, and Shaun decided it was time to let the general know where his package was, "Hey Ramon, did you get the package?"

"You haven't been here yet, my friend. Where are you?" he asked with anger in his voice.

"I had compass problems when we left Kingston, Ramon. Your package is trussed up on the beach across from Castillo de Morro," Shaun told him, "Do you want me to wait while you send some policia to check?"

Ramon laughed, "One of these days, O'Brien, I'm going to enjoy reading that somebody has finally killed you!"

"You'd miss me, Ramon, and you know it," Shaun laughed and ended the call, "Let's go home, boys. I can think of a couple of ways to spend my share of that bounty."

They all talked about the twenty thousand they'd earned for the night and reminisced about some of the other jobs that they had been together on, but the talk had a bittersweet tone as they realized for the first time that this was the end of the life that they had known under Henry and Shaun's leadership.

EPILOGUE

"Hey, Colonel," the younger man called into the room where a man in his late fifties was finishing the hated job of tying the perfect four-in-hand knot in the black tie that matched the suit, and his disposition.

"I'll be finished in a minute, has he arrived yet?" the Colonel asked.

"They say in about fifteen minutes, Sir. We need to go," the younger man in his early twenties was insistent.

"Tuck, I don't need you to tell me how to get dressed, or when to get to a funeral. Things are tough enough as it is, and I've attended too many!" He snapped.

"I understand, Sir. I'll just wait outside," the young man replied.

The older man looked in the mirror with astonishment at the old man looking back. His hair was close cropped in a military manner, but it failed to hide the baldness that had begun to set in ten years before, and the bags under his eyes gave him a perpetual look of sadness no matter what the occasion. Today should have been a celebration of his retirement, but another of his friends had died...too early by his estimation, but right on time in God's, of that he was certain. He brushed his teeth again out of nervousness and then walked out of the motel room to join Tuck in the car.

"I suppose we should go, although I wish we could just fish instead like we used to," he said to Tuck.

"Momma used to tell me stories about you and the men you ran around with 'back in the day', as she put it. What happened to them?" Tuck asked.

"Well, when you and Emily were little, you had lots of 'uncles', but the ones that you really took a shine to were Uncle Jerry and Uncle Mike. They took a contracting job in Africa about the time that the government decided to turn all the white farmers out and let the blacks take over the land. Both of them died in an IED explosion. Maggie's father, Shaun, finally succumbed to an old wound that he got when we rescued your Uncle Henry up in British Columbia. We don't hear from his wife very often, but I know that she was set on keeping the business in Barbados. The man we knew as Hurricane, Raleigh Evans, found Jesus and took over the old mission that Uncle Bob and Aunt Abigail ran down in Honduras. I heard that the congregation has tripled since he became pastor. Did I forget anybody?" He asked.

"Tell me what happened to Uncle Henry again," the young man said as they worked through traffic to the church.

"Well, Uncle Henry moved to Willow, Alaska shortly after he closed the business down. We used to see him regularly when he and your Aunt Avis would fly down to get out of the cold. Then one year we got a letter from Avis telling us that Henry had found a vein of gold and was going to work it through the winter. The story has it that when she went back up in the spring, she found him sitting in a dig, frozen stiff with a two-pound nugget in his hand and a smile on his face. Frozen up against him was his old Malamute, kind of like he was trying to warm Henry up...darndest thing, huh?" He told him.

"I guess it is. Why don't you write a book?" He asked.

"Nobody would believe it, for one thing, and for another, I've been to darn busy raising you and your sister," he replied with a smile, "Besides, being in charge of the men that I have under me has been a lot like raising somebody else's kids, so I really didn't have the time, although now might be a different story," the Colonel mused.

"Well, here we are, Dad. Are you ready for this?" the young man asked.

"I'm never ready to bury a friend and a brother, Tuck, but sometimes it is necessary. Can I tell you something while we can still talk?" He asked.

"Yes, Sir. We have time," Tuck answered.

"Your mother and I are very proud of what you have become, your sister too, of course, but especially you. Somewhere along the line, life got hold of us, and it didn't treat your mother kindly. I kind of turned away from God during that period, and never was able to really understand the kind of love that now shines through you. Who would ever have thought that the son of Michael Tucker would become a pastor of the church that his grandfather founded?" He told him with tears streaming down his face.

"When I was a little boy, Momma told Emily and I that you didn't have feelings like regular people, that you kept them bottled up inside all of the time. I think that probably isn't true anymore. Listen, Dad, I've got to go in, Momma's waiting with Aunt Maggie for me to speak to her before the service," Tuck told his father.

"I'll be there in a minute, Son. I just need to collect my thoughts so that I can give the eulogy," Tuck senior told him.

He sat in the car for a few minutes thinking about Amos, and how much he was going to miss him. Finally, he got out of the car and walked into the church where Emily, her husband, and Hanna were waiting for him.

"You look very handsome, Michael," Hanna kissed him on the cheek, and then took her handkerchief out and wiped the tears from his eyes, "When our son came through that door a few minutes ago, I thought that I'd gone back in time. He is the spitting image of you, Michael Tucker!"

"If it hadn't been for you, he might have turned out like me too! Praise God for that!" He laughed and kissed her cheek, careful not to smear her makeup.

The service was closed casket since Amos had wrecked his old biplane doing some stunt flying during his time off from the airline. Maggie was devastated, and Amos junior comforted his mother as they came back into the sanctuary of the church. Pastor Emeritus Bob Pike opened the service with prayer, and Abigail Pike, who still had a beautiful voice at seventy, sang the Lord's prayer. Michael Tucker junior stepped up to the podium and introduced his father when it came time for the eulogy, and Tuck senior made the long walk to the pulpit.

As he turned to face the gathering of friends and family of Amos Whitehorse, he looked across the pews and saw in a hazy way Henry, Shaun, Jerry, and Mike, standing in the back with their hands folded in front of them. For a minute he looked down at the lectern, and when he raised his head, they were no longer there. Tuck read the eulogy from a paper that he'd scribbled it on, not knowing exactly what words came out of his mouth, but when he finished, there wasn't a dry eye in the sanctuary. He stepped down to the casket, leaned over, and kissed the top.

"Goodbye old friend. I'll see you on the other side," he whispered, weeping.

Tuck then made his way slowly to the front row where Hanna sat with Maggie and sat between her and Emily who took his hand.

As he marveled at the young man preaching a short, but powerful sermon to close the service, Tuck heard Harry's voice in his head, "Don't regret the road that brought you here, Tuck. It also brought my grandson to that pulpit, and remember what I always told you, 'God works in mysterious ways'."

"He certainly does, Harry, He certainly does!" Tuck said under his breath.

The End.

ACKNOWLEDGEMENTS

I would like to thank my readers for their devotion to this series of novels.

Other Books by W.W. Brock:

COUGAR!

NIGHT WIND

THUNDER RANCH

TEXAS RISING

LEGION